ECHO OF BARBARA

Imprisoned for ten years, Sam Westwood had clung on by remembering his daughter Barbara. Now released, his main desire was to see her. However, Barbara detested her father's memory, and leaving her mother and her brother Roger at home, she had walked out and could not be found. But Roger had his own reason for wanting Barbara back: a wild scheme which, with the addition of Sam's old associates, would prove to have dangerous complications . . .

JOHN BURKE

ECHO OF BARBARA

Complete and Unabridged

LINFORD
Leicester

First published in Great Britain

First Linford Edition
published 2013

A catalogue record for this book is available
from the British Library.

ISBN 978–1–4448–1617–4

1

This was the day. Mrs. Westwood glanced at the clock a dozen times during breakfast. She did not really see what the time was: Roger would know when he had to leave, and there was no need for her to worry, but she could not stop those continual glances.

As soon as breakfast was over, Roger lit a cigarette. He smoked three, one after the other, and told his mother not to fidget.

'He won't want to be fussed when he gets back,' he said. 'For heaven's sake don't look so jumpy. Give him a chance to relax.'

'It's all very well for you to talk.' The bitter lines round her mouth grew darker. She seemed to be biting into her memories as though they were solid things. 'You don't know what it's like for me.'

'Take it easy,' he said. 'Just take it easy.'

He glanced, himself, surreptitiously at the clock.

'Don't you think,' said his mother, 'you ought to be starting out?'

The morning was still dark grey. The world beyond the window was limp with sea mist. Roger combed his hair, tugged at his jacket, and went into the hall for his coat. His mother followed him out. He knew she was going to speak, and knew what she was going to say.

It came in an abrupt, despairing rush. 'Don't you think, after all . . . perhaps there's no need to say too much about Barbara. I mean, not yet.'

'Don't let's go over all that again.'

'If we want him to settle down quietly, wouldn't it be better to keep quiet? Just for a bit, anyway. She may decide to come back — '

'She won't,' he said.

'I'm sure she will. Soon. And then he'd have been upset for nothing.'

Roger swung the car keys from his little finger. 'He's going to know the truth,' he said firmly, 'right from the start. We're not going to hold things back.'

Unexpectedly shrewd, she said: 'You want him to see who's let him down and

2

who hasn't, don't you?'

'I don't intend to cover up, that's all.'

'Don't overdo it. Your father's no fool.'

That did not even deserve an answer. Roger needed no telling about his father. He admired him and was proud in the gradually accumulated knowledge of what his father had done; and this was the day when they would come together again.

He kissed his mother on the cheek. She stood in the doorway and watched as he drove away. He did not look back. She did not wave.

The mist shrouded the sea from view. Here and there the haze was broken by the shape of one of the houses scattered along this stretch of coast. There was a faintly smoky smell in the air. Not until he was through the town and on the main road, climbing inland, did he emerge into pale sunshine. He accelerated. The car was small, but he had played with it until it gave him its best. When his father was back and they had their hands on all that hidden stuff, there would be a bigger car. Everything was going to be bigger and better.

He thought, sourly, of Barbara.

Well, this would show his father, if anything could. Barbara the pet, cherished and spoilt, doted on for all those years; Barbara, demonstrative and cloying . . . and now, at this moment of all moments, she was not here. She had failed.

'I'm not going to be there' — he could still hear her taut voice — 'when he gets out. I've stuck it until the last minute because of . . . because I wanted to keep things going. I wanted us to keep together.'

He had laughed derisively.

'You don't understand, do you?' she had said. 'I didn't want to leave Mother with you — with only you. But now you can all do without me. It's all going to start all over again; and I want no more of it.'

She had never forgiven her father. You could see that. It showed in her hostile eyes and in the way she brushed aside all protests. Not that Roger protested a great deal. Let her show herself in her true colours. It suited him well enough.

The road was deserted at this time of day. He could keep his foot down until he reached the outskirts of London. A puff of smoke from a train in the valley below kept level with him for a mile or two, then fell behind. A village closed in and dissolved again into the hedges.

He wondered what his father was feeling this morning, and what plans he was making.

'I don't want to be around when it starts again,' Barbara had said tensely. 'It'll be just the same — only this time we'll *know* . . . .The same old rackets. Living on stolen money, gradually getting things organized once more. Maybe' — her mouth had twisted — 'starting in a small way. Organizing the ice-cream vendors in that place you're going to — or even the donkeys on the shore. Fixing things.'

And so she had gone. Roger did not know where, and was not much concerned. He was pretty sure she would not come back: reluctantly, he granted her enough guts to do what she had said and not to retrace her steps.

The green miles dropped away behind and London began to reach out towards him. An electric train raced away from the country town which he had just skirted. A few lorries and private cars came out on the road. Before long the suburban streets were building up the pattern of their insoluble maze around him.

Roger glanced at the dashboard clock. He would make it comfortably.

The prison building looked almost warm in the sunlight. Its absurd turrets glowed a mellow brown, and a boy cycling past was whistling as though this were spring instead of autumn.

What was he going to say to his father? Roger had rehearsed no speech, no calculated welcome. He forced himself to sit back casually in the driver's seat, as though someone might be watching from one of those slits up there — someone who had to be impressed. The inevitable cigarette came out. He lit it deftly with one hand, and carefully relaxed. A man like his father, who had played that incredible cool-headed game all those years, would not want any fuss or awkwardness now, when he came out. He was going to find that he had a son he could trust — that the two of them were meant to work together.

Roger smoked his cigarette with a series of rhythmic gestures. He swung it up towards his mouth, poised it for a second, looked up at an angle as though smiling at some remote audience, and then opened his lips appreciatively. Every time he exhaled he smiled.

A small door in the great main door opened. A man came out with a suitcase in his right hand. The door closed behind him.

Roger sat very still for a moment, then opened the car door and got out.

His father looked very small. Roger had remembered him, somehow, as a tall, well-built man who dominated whatever company he was in. Now he was crushed by the gross building behind him.

He moved away from the door, and put one hand slowly up to his eyes, although the sun was not bright.

Roger cleared his throat. He felt cold. He said: 'Hello, Dad.'

Sam Westwood did not hesitate, but he did not quicken his pace. He advanced as though he were afraid that the earth might crumble beneath him; he was not quite steady on his feet.

At last their hands touched. There was no strength in Sam Westwood's grip.

'Hello, son.'

Roger opened the near-side door, took his father's case and put it in the back.

'It's a fine morning,' he said. 'Let's go, shall we?'

His father looked into the car. He said: 'I suppose Barbara's at home . . . waiting at home?'

2

Sam Westwood had shrunk. His whole face seemed to have sagged, and the pinkness of his cheeks had faded to a leathery yellow. There was no sign of that once-characteristic little swagger of his. Even sitting down, it used to be obvious: when he talked he would twitch his shoulders eagerly to and fro, as though striding along a road. And now his voice, too, had altered. It was little more than a whisper, like that of a man who had suffered from an attack of laryngitis and never recovered.

As they drove out of London he spoke little — only to ask: 'How's your mother?' and to comment: 'Nice little car, this.' Then, ten minutes later, he added: 'You've grown. I don't think I'd have recognized you. I suppose Barbara will have changed, too.'

It was the opening Roger needed, but he did not take it. Telling his father about

Barbara was going to be more difficult than he had realized. It was going to hurt.

'We'll stop for a drink when we get nearer home,' he said loudly and cheerfully.

There was no reply. His father was watching the countryside opening up on either side. What did it mean to a man who had not seen the outside world for ten years? The green trees and tilting fields . . .

Roger kept his eyes on the road as it wound through a straggling village and round a blind corner. It was silly to wonder about things like that. His father was probably thinking of something quite different. He was not likely to notice the scenery. Sam Westwood belonged to the city — to the throbbing city with its shining streets and clubs and restaurants, the places where men and women were bought and sold.

The silence was as chill and grey as the mist that had drifted across the sea early this morning. Roger had not expected it to be like this. He had expected his father to be jubilant, emerging at last from prison with all his old determination. He remembered him as a restless, exuberant man: and here was a shadow.

Roger began to talk. He talked too much, because he got so little response.

'I hope you'll like the house we picked out. I've seen better, but it's all right. And you did tell Mother that you wanted to be by the sea for a little while, didn't you?'

His father nodded abstractedly.

'Anyway, it'll do until you've decided what to do next.'

He waited. Just a hint of a plan would have been something to go on. His father would not have wasted his time in prison: he must have everything figured out.

There was no response.

Roger went on: 'I've got a couple of rooms in London, you know. I'm taking a week off to settle you in, and then I'll be seeing you maybe a couple of times a week. I'm in quite a nice little racket up there.'

His father turned and studied him curiously.

'My — er — associates,' said Roger with a knowing smile, 'think the world of you. Your name still means a lot, you know — in the right circles. They needle me a good bit — always asking why you didn't let me in on where you dumped that stuff.' His father's bleak, puzzled expression alarmed him suddenly. He hastened to add: 'But I knew you were right. You could have got word out to me — or anyone else, for that matter — but you wanted to work on your own, hm? You wanted to keep quiet until you could deal with the thing yourself.'

A bus came down the hill from a squat old church tower, and startled a hen that had been pecking at the roadside.

Sam Westwood watched it scurrying into the hedge. He made a noise in his throat that might have been a laugh.

'Mind you,' said Roger, 'I think my own bunch are pretty trustworthy. I've worked in with Lew Morrison off and on. He thinks you're the tops.'

'Stay away from Lew Morrison,' said his father, not turning to look at him.

'All right, all right.' Roger made it sound bright and happy. 'Sure, Dad. Now you're back, I'm in with any set-up you want. It's just that I've been finding my way around. You know how it is.' He stopped, and again there was silence. He plunged into it. 'Mind you, it's been hard going sometimes. We could have done with some of that haul of yours. Even Mother said — '

'And Barbara?'

Roger braked for a turning. The road went over a bridge and through a small town. Traffic was brisk now. It gave him an excuse for not replying for a couple of minutes. When they came out the other side, his father's harsh whisper came again:

'And Barbara? How did she feel about it?'

Then Roger told him. Barbara was gone. Barbara had hardly ever mentioned her father's name while he was away; when she did, it was to express disgust. The ten-year-old who had been Daddy's darling had reached the twenties, and her love had not lasted. He spoke more savagely than he had intended; the memory of his father's preference for Barbara, and the injustice of it, rose with an irresistible pressure that forced the words out.

13

Then it was over. The truth was spoken. Sam Westwood said nothing.

His only sign of life came when the car emerged from the trees above the saltings and dipped down towards the twisting creeks that broadened into the sea. Then he leaned slightly forward. He stared down at the water. The land swayed slowly ahead of them, flattening as they reached the level. Now the town was an untidy huddle on their right, leaking away into a spattering of houses and bungalows.

The car turned away from the town. Sam Westwood looked out at the houses near the sea. There was no apparent enquiry in his gaze. He simply looked. His expression did not change when the car stopped outside the isolated house which stood close to the first yellow line of shingle.

'Well,' said Roger, 'here we are.'

His father got out and stood for a moment by the car as though needing its shelter. Then he lifted his eyes slowly, narrowing them against the shrouded grey brightness of the autumn sky.

14

The door of the house opened. Sam Westwood moved towards his wife.

She did not run to meet him. Her smile was speculative and at the same time nervous. Roger, coming behind his father, could have groaned; nearly did groan aloud, in fact. The quietness, the deadness of it all . . . His mother looked more as though she were about to whine about being left alone for ten years than to welcome her husband home.

Sam Westwood put his arms round her and held her for a long time. She remained stiff and unsure of herself: she looked enquiringly into his face as soon as he released her.

'So this is the place,' said Sam in that new, disconcerting whisper of his.

'This is it,' Roger took him up. 'Nothing wonderful, but you can put your feet up for a while. And then — well, we'll see, won't we?'

He gripped his father's arm and smiled. There was no responsive movement. The arm felt as though all strength had gone out of it.

It was all too quiet. The homecoming

was drab and meaningless. You'd have thought a man getting out of prison would have wanted to talk and sing and shout — would have wanted to have a few days in town with lights, noise, music . . .

Maybe that would come. Soon that would come.

'As soon as you feel like it,' Roger tried, knowing that soon it must all come right, 'we'll go and have an evening in the town here. Not much of a dump, but you find quite a good crowd there at weekends. Anyone with any initiative could build the place up' — he winked — 'in all sorts of ways.'

Even the donkeys on the shore, murmured a stupid echo in his mind. He blotted it out.

His father would not sit down. He kept moving across the small room to and from the window, looking out at the tough spiky grass and the shingle, then turning away — and turning back abruptly, as though he might catch the mirage dissolving.

Distantly, it might have been to himself, he said: 'All those people, on top of you . . . the weight of them all round

16

you and over you and under you.'

Time, thought Roger. It would take time. He must be patient. His father had got to have time to find out how well he could be trusted; take it easy, and let him get used to being out in the world again, and it would all work out fine.

★ ★ ★

'Walking,' said Sam Westwood: 'funny — I never seemed to do much walking, did I?' His voice was as hushed and hoarse as the persistent voice of the sea on the shingle. 'And going out fishing — that's something special, I've heard.'

He gave the impression of experimenting timidly with life. Roger found that his company was not wanted. His father preferred to stroll aimlessly across the saltings alone. If he ever went into the town, he did not mention it. When he did make a friend, it was a leathery, taciturn old fisherman who took him out in a battered trawler. From these trips on foot or afloat he returned with no sign of having enjoyed himself: he described nothing, commented

17

on nothing, asked no questions; he could have been quietly content or utterly indifferent.

Roger imposed patience on himself. It was difficult. The last few months, as the day of his father's release grew closer, had been tiring: they had been tolerable only because of the thought that when the day came everything would be sorted out. And now this was his father — this drained, withdrawn creature.

Time. Give him time.

A week away in London, thought Roger, and on his return he would find his father slowly changing. He would relax, grow more expansive, realize that he was free again. Not right away, of course. Next weekend . . . or the one after . . .

And then the one after that, and yet another.

Still there was no change. Sam Westwood was courteous to his wife, and helped about the house. He smiled when Roger returned from London, and patted him abstractedly on the shoulder. For hours in the evening he would listen to the radio, though with an air of detachment that made one doubt whether he heard anything. He might almost have been waiting for something — filling in time, waiting with unwavering calm for some plan to mature or someone to appear.

But nobody knew he was here. He had been most insistent about that before he left prison. No one was to know.

Because he wanted peace and quiet — or because he was afraid?

Roger did not believe that his father was afraid. Even now, seeing him as only a shadow of his former self, he was sure that fear had nothing to do with this deliberate seclusion. Somewhere, somehow, a plan was maturing: it must be.

Yet nothing happened. Sam Westwood said nothing and did nothing about that fabulous haul which had caused all the trouble and cut all those prison years out of his life.

3

The car had sprung a flat tyre some miles outside London. Roger was late arriving at the studio, and felt hot and greasy as he went up the stairs.

A girl passed him, coming down. She was a silver blonde, heavily perfumed and frozen in make-up. She glanced at him once, and angrily looked away again. Her heels struck against the treads of the stairs, then set up a new, more impatient rhythm as she reached ground level.

Roger pushed open the door at the top of the stairs and went through. There were three girls sitting on the chairs against the wall in the little corridor that had been converted into a waiting-room. They looked up expectantly. One gave him a red smile and said: 'Good morning, Mr. Westwood.'

'Good morning,' he said, and went on.

The large room beyond was hot with arc lamps. A girl wearing shorts and a pink brassière leaned against a metal screen. A young man going bald stood by one of the cameras and said, 'Not bad,' then said, 'Hello, Roger,' then, to the girl, said, 'Lean forward. Mm. Yes, I reckon you'll do.'

Roger went round the screen and into the tiny office behind it.

Stan Morrison looked up from a heap of bromides and scowled. 'Thought you'd gone off with your old man to collect the treasure.'

Roger tried to shrug unconcernedly. 'Not yet.'

'When's it going to be?'

'You sound pretty foul this morning,' Roger protested. He had expected the usual challenge, and expected it to be more savage than the last time or the time before; but he had not been prepared for such an immediate attack. 'What's the matter?' he ventured. 'Did that blonde on the stairs spit in your eye, or something?'

It was closer to the truth than he had guessed. 'That blonde,' Stan growled: 'you saw which one she was?'

'Just looked like one of the usuals.'

'She was the one we used in the last two issues of *Damsel*.'

'The one — '

'The one my old man had his eye on,' Stan Morrison sourly agreed. 'But she won't play. She won't even have those other pictures taken — you know, the breakdown stage — and if she won't go that far, she's no good for the Morrison stable.'

That was a tested scientific fact: the models who drew back from the prospect of posing for some of the periodicals with a more limited sale — yet a more remunerative one — never enjoyed the prospect of joining Lew Morrison's chorus.

Roger picked up the morning mail, which Stan had pushed to one side of his desk, and began to go through it. He said:

'Well, there are plenty more where she came from. And your father's got plenty to be going on with.'

'My father's got where he is,' said Stan fiercely, 'from never letting up. He keeps at it. A good thing for us, too — '

'Of course,' Roger hastened to say, aware of what was inevitably coming.

'If it was left to you and your promises, we wouldn't have much of a future to look forward to.'

'It wouldn't be bad,' Roger attempted. 'We're doing nicely — '

'Not as nicely as you said you would. It was all going to expand when your old man came out of stir — that's what you promised. Plenty of backing from him, and plenty of scope for building up the business. Well, where's the backing?'

Roger said stiffly: 'He's . . . not ready yet. Not ready to talk.'

'Christ,' said Stan.

He pouted like a girl: he had a dark face that was almost Italian, and a heavy lower lip that drooped petulantly. When he was alone in the room he would smoke a cigarette that dangled from one corner of his mouth, held by that moist lip, and study himself in the glass on the wall. When other people were with him he would wave the cigarette constantly between two fingers. Roger had copied Stan's mannerisms with a cigarette until he had developed some of his own.

Someone banged into the metal screen

outside the office, cursed, and put his head round the door.

'Don't forget those three outside,' he said. 'Especially Maisie. Maisie's ripe for the picking, if you ask me.'

'All right, Archie, all right.' Stan leaned back in his chair, already seeming to swell into the plump, smooth operator that his father was. 'Send her in first.'

The two of them waited in silence. They were partners, but gradually they were becoming enemies. If Roger did not soon produce the promised results, Stan would really get down to hating him.

A brunette was shown in. She said, 'Good morning, Mr. Morrison,' and, for the second time, 'Good morning, Mr. Westwood.'

Roger sat on the edge of the desk. He felt better. It was at moments like these that he was conscious of power. Yet there was also the thrill of being unsure — of gambling on girls like these, not knowing whether they would turn out right, whether one's judgement had been sound.

He said: 'You've done some good work for us, Maisie.'

'It's not work,' she said with a cool, self-satisfied laugh. 'Just displaying what I've been given' — she glanced downwards almost coyly — 'isn't much. Or is it?' Her lips parted, and she looked straight at Roger.

'You've enjoyed working with us, haven't you, Maisie?' said Stan.

'Sure thing. And it's nice to see my . . . face . . . on the bookstalls.' Again the laugh.

The two young men looked at her for a long minute. Then Roger swung half round and nodded. Stan dipped into one of the desk drawers, took out a magazine, and tossed it across the desk. Maisie stared down at it, and began slowly to smile. She picked it up and opened it.

They watched her face. Still she was smiling.

'This is hot stuff, isn't it?' she said at last.

'It pays well,' said Roger quietly.

'It'd need to.' She passed the magazine back.

Stan said: 'Well?'

'Well?' she echoed.

25

'The distribution of this sort of thing is tricky, but we have regular customers who pay through the nose for it. The trouble is, they're always wanting something new. Somebody new,' he added.

'Jaded appetites, eh?' said Maisie cheerfully.

Roger relaxed. She was hooked. He and Stan had not been wrong.

He said: 'You'd like to earn bigger money?'

'Who wouldn't?'

Roger slipped from the desk. 'Come and see Archie,' he said. 'Maybe he's got some time for a little shooting this morning. Just to get you used to it.'

He delivered the girl to the cameraman, and then came back.

Stan ought to have been looking pleased, but he was not. His expression was the same as it had been when Roger first entered the office this morning. He went back to the attack.

'So there's still nothing doing? What the hell does your old man think he's playing at?'

'He knows what he's doing,' said Roger defensively.

26

'Does he? That's nice to know. I wish *I* knew what he's doing, that's all. When you think of what we could do with more capital — more apparatus, better distribution facilities, getting our stuff into the foreign movie market . . . Just when are we going to get that money, that's what I'm asking.'

Roger had been asking it too; not out loud, but over and over again in his head. But all he could say was: 'It's all going to be all right.'

Stan began to speak very slowly. It was unusual for him — unnatural, in fact. 'I came into this business with you,' he said deliberately, 'because I'd heard a lot about your father. All about what a smart operator he was, until he got caught. And even then, they said — *you* said — he was smart enough to keep his hands on the stuff. It was there waiting for him when he came out, you said. We'd cut in on it, you said. With Sam Westwood behind us, there were terrific possibilities. Well, he's out now: where's the stuff?'

'Can't you shut up for just one minute?' snapped Roger. 'My father makes his own mind up about things. When he's good and ready, I'll be the first to hear.'

'You think so?'

'I'm sure of it,' said Roger, sounding more confident than he felt.

'If there's anything there at all,' said Stan meaningly.

'What do you mean by that?'

'What do you think I mean? Has your father really got that stuff safe somewhere? Maybe one of the others got away with it after all . . . '

'No.' Roger denied it swiftly, denying it fervently to himself at the same time.

'Well, that's the way it looks. That's the way I'm beginning to think. And my old man, too — he's not so sure about the set-up.'

A woman laughed outside. There came the deeper, answering rumble of men's laughter. Stan glanced instinctively towards the door, and the vicious lines in his face softened. He sighed, and pushed himself up from his chair.

'Better go and check there's some work going on,' he said.

He pushed past Roger.

Roger said: 'It's not just the cash — not just the future. You're getting a hell of a kick out of this place as it is, and you know it. And if it hadn't been for me you wouldn't be in on it.'

Stan stood for a moment at the door, looking into the studio. His lips curled appreciatively. Over his shoulder he said in a milder voice, but one that had not lost its scepticism: 'Your job is to get some more money into our hands. Fast. It's time we saw some results.'

Then he sauntered out.

Roger, watching him go, wanted to kill him. Or at any rate to bring him to his knees. He wanted to be in a position to telephone someone, to mutter curt instructions, and to know that Stan Morrison would be picked up and dealt with. That was the way his father had done things. No one had insulted Sam Westwood and got away with it. Sam Westwood had been respected and omnipotent.

Maybe if he knew what young scum like that were saying about him . . .

★ ★ ★

Instead of staying in London for a full week, Roger drove down to Easterdyke the next morning.

It was a cold day. The wind smacked at the side of the car as he approached the sea along the road that swung slowly round in an arc before dipping towards the sea. Getting out in front of the house, he felt the bleakness in the air, and thought of the warm office in London. His father must be mad to have suggested living here, even temporarily.

His footsteps in the poky hall brought his mother and father out.

'You didn't say you'd be back so soon,' his mother complained.

His father looked past him, as though expecting someone else to be there. But Roger had closed the door, and there was nobody there.

Sam Westwood said faintly: 'I thought you might have . . . that is, I wondered . . .'

'That's all you think about,' said his wife. 'The rest of us don't count. Just because Barbara isn't here, nothing counts.'

He touched her arm gently but without real meaning. She twitched away and went out into the kitchen.

Roger said: 'You're not still hoping Barbara will come back, are you? I told you, the mood she was in, she wasn't intending to come back. It's no good, Dad.'

He went in and stood by the fire. The wind moaned thoughtfully to itself around the exposed house, and there was a noticeable draught from somewhere around the window-frame.

Sam Westwood returned to his chair.

'None of your friends have seen her?' he asked.

'No.'

'You could ask them to look out for her. If you really went about it — '

'We wouldn't find her if she didn't want to be found,' said Roger.

Sam did not seem to hear. He held his hands out in front of him and flexed the fingers as though trying their strength. Distantly he said:

'What *is* this business of yours?'

Roger felt a quiver of excitement. This

was the first sign of interest his father had shown. Perhaps this was the opening he had been waiting for; perhaps, at last, the shell was beginning to crack.

'It's a pretty slick little organization,' he said, moving to the chair opposite his father. 'We started out supplying photographs — pin-up stuff, you know — to magazines. Then we began to publish our own magazine. You have to go carefully, but once you know the ropes you can't miss.'

'Pornography?' said his father mildly.

'Well, you know the sort of thing. We've got several monthly ones going now — good glossy art paper, high-class stuff — and one or two for private circulation if you know what I mean.'

'I know what you mean.'

'We've got the market pretty well sewn up,' said Roger expansively. 'All we need now is more capital. Then we can expand.'

'Expand?' said Sam Westwood. His expression was as remote as his rustling voice. 'There's no future in that sort of thing. Small-time dirt. You'll never make a fortune out of that.'

Roger flushed. He wavered, on the verge of making a sharp retort; but it wasn't worth it — not now, with his father at last showing *some* interest. Stiffly he said:

'We've explored the possibilities thoroughly. I don't think you know just how you can branch out in this racket. There are side issues — '

'Such as keeping Lew Morrison supplied with girls?'

'I never mentioned Lew Morrison.'

'You did,' said Sam Westwood, 'when you drove me down, a few weeks ago. And the only reason Lew Morrison would even bother to smile at a little operator like you is that you're channelling raw material into his clubs.'

Still Roger kept his temper. Still he held the words on a level, like someone practising one note over and over again — a steady, dead note without vibrato.

'We don't turn down useful contacts,' he said. 'Morrison or anyone else, they all widen your scope.'

'But you're still not big enough,' said his father, fingers locking together and stiffening, 'to find your own sister.'

They were back. The important topic receded; the shadow of that spoilt, stuck-up creature darkened the room again.

Roger said again: 'If she didn't want to be found, nobody could — '

'In my day,' said his father, 'it could have been done. I'd have found her. I'd have found anybody.'

It was too much. The anger was like a bitter vomit that could not be kept in any longer. Roger got up from his chair. He stood above his father, dominating the crumpled little figure. He shouted:

'In *your* day. I've been living on your day for a long time, and it's been a big mistake. I've been waiting for you to come back, and now look. Look at you!'

'I'm sorry,' whispered his father. It was a brittle, mocking whisper. 'I'm sorry I didn't come back in splendour with machine-guns blazing. That's what you wanted, isn't it?'

'All I wanted,' cried Roger, 'was for you to let me in with you. To . . . to trust me.'

'Trust you?'

'Where's the stuff you lifted?' In his own head, resounding, Roger heard the plaintive echoes of his own despairing appeal. 'If you'd come through with that — share it, let me in on it — give me a chance to use it, instead of sitting there sneering at me and the work I'm doing, that'd be something. And all the time I get cracks made at me . . . Do you know what they say about you? Do you know? And me having to stand and take it.'

Sam Westwood stood up. Roger took an instinctive step backwards. Sam grinned a slight, wintry grin.

'We'd better try to understand one another, son. I never made a habit of telling anybody anything. I'm not going to start now. That's the way it always was, and that's how it is now.'

Roger followed him impotently to the door. 'Damn you.' He could have burst into tears. 'How long is this going to go on?'

'It's a nice, crisp day,' said Sam. 'I think I'll have a breath of air.'

'What's the game?' cried Roger. 'What's it all about? If you muffed the job — if you never got the diamonds after all . . . '

His father did not even look round.

* * *

Mrs. Westwood crossed the room and meaninglessly plumped up the couch cushions.

'Yes,' she said; 'that's how he's been with me, too. All the time. I've been hanging on all these years telling myself everything would go back to what it was before. And it's all meant nothing — all the waiting.'

There was no real need for her to tell him this. He knew it all. He had known since he was a boy what she felt. It was all there in her tart comments on life as it was then and in her blustering assurance as to what it would be later. Later, when things went back to normal. No alternative was possible: she was waiting for the rich bright world to be laid at her feet again, as Aladdin's stolen palace had at last returned under the Sultan's window.

For Roger it had been the same. He, too, had waited. But for him there had been no bitterness, no spasms of rage against the man who had so skilfully concealed his true profession for so long.

Sam Westwood's son had grown up to admire and envy him: no father returning from heroic action in a noble war had been more eagerly awaited than Sam Westwood after his ten years in prison.

Wife and son — alike, wanting the same things, yet not united and not devoted to one another. They did not talk a lot: they pursued their own dreams and planned their own futures. They were simply fellow prisoners, linked only by their need for that other prisoner to be released at last and to come to them, releasing them in their turn.

' . . . a house fit to call a house,' she lamented, 'and a life worth living. It wasn't too much to ask. I've been patient. You can't say I haven't been patient. Hanging about all these years, after the sort of life we'd been used to — and now this!'

The clouds over the sea thickened, and although this was morning a sombre twilight crept into the room.

Roger said: 'He must have it somewhere. If he hadn't got it, he'd have said so outright.'

'You can't even be sure of that. To think that I stood by him and — '

'He's got to crack up sooner or later. No man in his right mind could leave all that lying around, wherever it is — just lying there — and not go to pick it up.'

'In his right mind,' echoed his mother hopelessly.

'If we could get him back to some of his old haunts, he'd see sense,' urged Roger, as though by persuading her he could move his father. 'He needs to live as he used to live — '

'We had so much. So much.' She was grey with her own wretchedness: it was impossible to tell how much she had said to her husband when they were alone together, how vainly she had talked and how little he had replied. Abruptly she said: 'The only person he would tell is Barbara. If she were here. And if she'd ask him.'

'Which she wouldn't,' growled Roger.

'She's the only one. If only you could find her and talk to her. Maybe that's all it is. Being in prison does things to a man — makes him queer. You've only got to look at him to see that. Barbara's all he wants. And the way he is now, Barbara's the only one he'd tell.'

Roger nodded slowly. 'Yes,' he said. 'She's the only one. If we could find Barbara . . . '

4

Spread out all over the floor and on the desk, back issues of Pepper Publications looked as dull and unappetizing as a heap of ancient parish magazines.

Stan Morrison glanced into the office, cursed, and said: 'Hurry up and get that bloody mess cleared up, will you? I want to sit down sometime.'

Roger skimmed through yet another issue, and flung it aside. Automatically he reached for the nearest one to hand. Had he already gone through this? It looked just the same as all the others; he had lost the ability to distinguish between them. Girls on their knees thrust flimsily covered breasts at him; 'artistic' poses exhibited a tangle of legs and hunched shoulders; the repetitive patterns of arched eyebrows, breasts, navels, and knees were tiring his eyes.

Actually — it would have been a laugh to anyone who was told this — he was looking for a face. One particular, half-remembered face.

He got up from the floor, his legs stiff. On the desk was a small pile he had not yet investigated. He picked up the top magazine and leafed through it. Nothing in there. Then there were several consecutive issues. He opened the first; and there she was.

Roger sighed. He opened the pages out and tossed the magazine to the other side of the desk. The girl stared up at the ceiling. Roger turned away, then turned back abruptly as though to catch the photograph by surprise. Then he studied it at length, closely and at a distance.

He had been right. She would do.

Stan Morrison came in as he was gathering up the copies from the floor.

'Found what you were looking for?'

'Yes,' said Roger jubilantly.

'Thank God for that. What was it — don't tell me you're getting interested in women after all this time? I thought they were rather out of your line.'

Roger stifled an instinctive retort. He could take that sort of remark now.

Instead, he jerked his thumb towards the open magazine. 'Who's that?'

Stan shrugged. 'No idea.'

'Those issues are a year old. We don't seem to have used her since then. But I've got to find her.'

'What's all the fuss about?' demanded Stan.

Roger almost decided to tell him. But the plan might fail. It was a long chance, and if it failed there would be more jeers, more savage contempt. Let him wait.

Roger said: 'It's a personal matter. I must talk to this girl. Tell you all about it later.'

His curiosity aroused, Stan picked up the glossy photograph and studied it more carefully. He pursed his lips. He had a good memory: like his father, he remembered women. When you lived on women, you needed to know all and remember all.

'Yes,' he said thoughtfully. 'Dark brown hair. Very smooth skin.' His eyes narrowed appreciatively, as though smoke had drifted into them. 'Very smooth. And grey eyes — very light grey.'

'That's her.'

'It's coming back to me now. She came to London to be an actress — '

'Perfect! Couldn't be better.'

Stan was pulling open the top drawer of the filing cabinet. 'A hell of a lot of 'em do that. Let's see, what issue was it? Mm.' He pulled out a file, and went on fitting pieces together in his mind. 'She was one of those who went on.'

'To your father's?'

'I think so.' Stan took out a card. 'Paula Hastings. Yes, she was the one all right — she went on to one of the clubs. I'll give the old man a tinkle, and locate her.'

Roger collected the remaining magazines and stacked them in the cupboard. He was hardly aware of the movements of his hands as he prodded the last one into place and closed the cupboard door. All his attention belonged on Stan, perched on the desk with the receiver in his left hand, whistling through his teeth.

'That you, Pop? Listen . . . '

If she had gone on to Lew Morrison, maybe she would not be the right sort of girl. It was hard to imagine her playing the part he had devised for her. And

43

anyway, with the sort of money and the sort of life she would be used to by now, what chance was there that she'd be interested?

He listened to Stan's questions, listened to the answering crackle in the receiver. Stan's eyes rested on him, cold and sardonic. Stan said: 'Is that so? Well, we've got plenty more where that one came from.' The metallic voice went on for a few seconds and then ceased. Stan put the telephone down.

Roger said: 'Well?'

'She doesn't work there any more. She didn't like it. And my old man doesn't like to be reminded of her, much.'

'Where did she go?'

'Pop told me,' said Stan blandly, 'where he thought she ought to have gone.'

Roger held out his hand. Stan dropped the file card into it.

'She may not live there any longer,' he said.

'I'll find out,' said Roger.

★　★　★

The girl frowned into her glass of Dubonnet and swung it gently to and fro so that the ice clinked against the sides. Her hair was longer than it had been in the photograph. Her eyes looked tired, rimmed with a languid, rather noble darkness. She wore no jewellery, and the flesh of her throat had a shadowy richness that was more disturbing than all the exposed bodies in all the magazine pictures.

She said: 'I don't want to have anything to do with Lew Morrison again.'

'This is a private matter,' said Roger. 'It concerns me, and only me. Morrison doesn't come into it.'

'If you're still a partner of that son of his — '

'This is separate,' said Roger. 'You won't be concerned with the Morrisons at all.'

She drank, and put her glass down. Her eyes, sunk in darkness, were a velvety grey — soft, yet startlingly clear and demanding.

'I'm not fussy about many things nowadays,' she said; 'but your precious friend taught me to be more critical than

I thought I could be. That's why I'm where I am now. That's why I'm even listening to you — because once he'd made me really sick, and I'd walked out, he saw to it that I didn't get a job anywhere else. Powerful friends you have.'

He sensed that her language was not her own. This was not the way she spoke when she was truly herself: it was the tongue of the world which she had entered a year ago . . . two years? . . . some time back. He knew because he was like that himself. It was the way things went nowadays. You said what you meant in phrases from the cinema, and it sounded good, and after a while everyone was talking like that and it became almost natural and ceased to be an act any longer. *Powerful friends you have . . .*

He said: 'I don't have to run with the Morrisons. My father' — he was approaching the point of this interview — 'is bigger than a dozen types like Morrison.'

'If he's in the same line of business — '

'No,' said Roger. 'He wouldn't touch that sort of thing. He never needed to.'

She watched him, waiting. He was

conscious of a tingle of optimism. Her calm, sceptical self-possession was just right. If she would listen — if she would only agree — it would all work out just as he had planned.

He went on: 'I'll tell you the whole story. In confidence. I'll have to trust you.' He waited for some acknowledgement. She made no comment; did not move. 'Another drink?' he said.

'Thank you, no. Tell me what you want.'

'My father,' he said, 'is Sam Westwood. Just over ten years ago he was a very respectable citizen. Very respectable indeed. We had a large house, in its own grounds, beyond Maidenhead. Two cars, a boat — everything.' He thought of the boat and of the gentle plash of water and the way the lawn ran down to the river. 'My father,' he said, 'drove into London most mornings, and came back sometimes in the early evening, sometimes late. We understood he was a promoter of some sort — Westwood Enterprises, his firm was called, and somehow we got the idea over the years that he had a finger in every pie in the entertainment business.

47

My mother sometimes asked him what he was doing, and he'd say that he had been involved in a big deal over theatre scenery, or had been trying to do something to get restrictions lifted in some big restaurants. Post-war rationing — you remember? It seems a long time ago.'

'I wasn't much more than a kid. Just a little,' she judicially added, 'older than you, I suppose.'

The calm assumption of superiority annoyed him. 'You can't be all that much older.'

'Twenty-three,' she said.

'That's just right.'

'Right for what?'

'My sister,' he said, 'is twenty-three.'

She stared.

He said: 'My sister Barbara was always my father's pet. She was brought up to consider herself the most wonderful thing that ever existed. Nothing was too good for her. Dad spent most of his spare time with her. They were always hanging about together. But when it came down to it — when she discovered what he'd really been up to . . . '

'Well?'

'She's not like me,' he said passionately. 'She wanted all the trimmings — she couldn't take the truth underneath.'

Paula Hastings said: 'I don't know what all this is about.'

'I'd better go back and tell you the rest of the story. Just over ten years ago we found out that Dad wasn't as respectable as he looked. He was a big shot in the — er — '

'The crime world,' she supplied flatly.

'He was smart, that was all,' snapped Roger. 'He wanted the good things, and he knew how to get them. He didn't get mixed up in any of the smaller things — other people did those jobs for him. The police never got anywhere near him.' His enthusiasm kindled. The picture that had been built up in his mind over these years came to life again; he marvelled at the empire which his father had ruled. 'Everything was running smoothly. But on one big job my father decided to go along himself.'

'Why?'

Roger had asked himself that question

so often, and every time there was a different answer. He tried now to sound confident and mysterious. 'It was something really big. He couldn't have trusted even his best men. He wanted to supervise the whole thing. When it was the big stuff, he had to deal with it personally.'

Paula was watching his mouth. She said: 'You're crazy about your father, aren't you?'

'I've been waiting ten years for him to get out.'

'This last job of his you've been talking about — '

'He got on to something terrific. The biggest haul ever. The Mannerlaw diamonds.'

At last he had made an impression on her. She let out a faint, wondering sigh. 'I've heard about them.'

'A lot of people have heard about them,' he said proudly. 'A lot of people would like to know where they are.'

'Your father was the man who went to prison — I remember hearing someone talking about him.'

Roger held himself back for a moment. He tried to sit quite still and study the girl. He needed a quick, final assessment before he gambled on her.

He said: 'You do want a job, don't you? And a lot of money.'

'I wouldn't even have come to meet you if I didn't.'

He was almost prompted to drop some sinister hint about his own contacts, and the things that might happen to her if she cheated him; but the look in her eyes stopped him in time.

'If you turn down the offer I'm going to make you,' he said carefully, 'you'll keep quiet about it afterwards?'

'Plenty of things have happened to me that I don't talk about,' she said. 'This won't be any different.'

He was still studying her face. The longer he looked at it, the stronger the resemblance became.

'All right,' he said at last. 'My father got the Mannerlaw diamonds. Quite a while after the war ended. The family collection — paintings, jewellery, everything — had been moved out of London to the country home of some relative. The old earl went with it. When his son got back from the war, their London place was cleaned up and all the treasures were disinterred from the country and brought back. At least, that was the idea.' He could not repress a smile. The terrific idea, the planning, the way it had been carried out . . . He said: 'The Mannerlaw diamonds were travelling in a car with two private detectives. It was all very inconspicuous — all carefully worked out and very secret. Only there weren't such things as secrets where my father was concerned. He knew too many people, without them realizing it. He knew every detail, and knew where and how to make the snatch. It was the fastest hold-up you ever heard of — all over in less than a minute.'

'But,' she said, 'they were caught.'

The triumph ebbed out of Roger's voice. 'Yes,' he said; 'they were caught.' The memory of treachery was like a sour taste in his mouth. 'One of the three men with him squealed. There was a row over the shareout of the proceeds — that's what everyone who knew about it says. It got into all the papers after the trial

— headlines like 'Thieves fall out' and that sort of dirt. The men wanted a bigger cut, and my father stuck to what he'd arranged. There was a big split, and a rough-house somewhere one evening. The police got to hear of it and pulled one of the men in. They must have worked him over pretty thoroughly. Told him one of the detectives they'd attacked was likely to die and he'd be charged with murder, or something like that. Anyway, he talked. They pulled my father in, and eventually they got the other two.'

And so the house, the garden, the river, the cars, the fine days all came to an end. After the trial and the conviction for robbery with violence, there was still enough money for them to exist on while they waited; but it was existence, not life.

Paula Hastings said: 'But the Manner-law diamonds — they never got them back, did they?'

Roger drew a deep breath. 'That's the point.'

'Your father — '

'The quarrel between him and his men was because he refused to share out. He paid them for the job, and that was that. It was the way he always worked. And he hid the diamonds before the police caught up with him. Nobody knows where.'

Wonderingly she shook her head. Impersonal voices buzzed around them, but he and the girl might have been in a different world. He took her empty glass from between her slim fingers. She sat with her legs crossed, apparently contemplating her right foot.

She said: 'And the rest of you really didn't know about your father? I mean, your mother must have known what he was up to.'

'No, she didn't know. Right to the end she thought Dad worked in an office, running a respectable business. She played bridge and gave little parties, and she was always spending money, and she was happy.'

'And now,' said Paula, 'you can all spend money again, I suppose? I mean, he must be out by now, surely?'

Tersely, bitterly, Roger told her the truth. He admitted to her, as he could not have admitted to Stan Morrison, the humiliation he had been suffering since his father was freed. There was no holding back now. Those dispassionate, quietly challenging grey eyes released his pent-up anger and frustration: they encouraged him in a way he could not explain. It was almost as though he had some tangled sin to confess. When he had explained everything, and she had replied, there would be assuagement.

He finished. She had not touched her drink all the time he was speaking. Now she said:

'Yes. Ironic, isn't it? But what has it got to do with me?'

'There's only one person he might talk to,' said Roger. He forced himself to slow down now; forced himself to drive his words heavily, methodically home. 'The thing that's hit him most — the only thing that's affected him in any way since he came out, as far as we can see — has been Barbara's disappearance. If she were to come back, I believe he'd give way. *She* could coax it out of him.'

She laughed briefly, disbelievingly. 'And

I . . . I'm like your sister: is that it?'

'Yes,' said Roger; 'that's it.'

A man passed them carrying three pint tankards with his two hands clasped around them in a praying gesture. Somebody began to laugh hysterically behind a pillar in the middle of the bar. Roger and Paula had hunched towards one another, their voices low. They might have been lovers, murmuring together — or tensely quarrelling.

Paula said: 'You must be mad. He knows his own daughter — '

'After ten years? He remembers what Barbara was like ten years ago. She's changed a lot since then, and he'll be expecting her to have changed. You look like someone who could have grown up from what Barbara was then.'

For a moment she looked intolerably sad. The shadows ran like tears down her cheeks as she moved her head away from the mellow light above her. She lifted one hand as though to brush away the cobweb of a dream.

'He'd know at once,' she insisted. 'If they were as close as you say, there must have been all sorts of little things — catch-phrases, pet names, places they went to and jokes they had together . . . '

'I remember most of them,' said Roger. He had listened to so many of their shared jokes, their walled intimacy, and stored them up in his memory. They had sharp, hurtful edges; he could recapture every detail clearly. 'Maybe there are one or two I've forgotten, or never heard of. But you'd be bound to have forgotten them yourself, anyway — Barbara, I mean. I can give you enough to be convincing.'

'It couldn't possibly work. Do you mean he hasn't seen her, or a photograph, or anything?'

'He didn't want her to visit him in prison,' said Roger. 'He thought too much of her — didn't want to upset her, even when she was old enough to face up to such things. And even if he had wanted her to visit him' — his lip curled — 'she wouldn't have gone.'

Again there was silence between them.

Abruptly the girl said: 'I don't like the sound of your sister. Or maybe it's just the way you put it. Maybe — '

'Put it any way you like,' he said; 'she was a bitch. A weak, dismal snob. When I think of how she used to hang around him — all the fuss, all the cuddling and giggling and all the rest of it . . . If that was love — really, honestly, I mean — then why couldn't she . . . '

There was no need to finish. Anyway, there were no words keen and destructive enough. He shrugged his contempt. And Paula Hastings said:

'You think I'm like her?'

'I say you look like her. Enough like her for me to have noticed. Certainly enough for my father to think that you're Barbara. The rest will be a matter of acting.'

'What would happen,' she demanded wryly, 'if she came back while I was in the middle of the act?'

'She won't.'

'And afterwards — when it's all over . . . ?'

'When we've got the money,' said Roger, 'you can walk out again. I can promise you a comfortable share. You can take it, and go. You can throw a fit of temper: you can say all the things Barbara said about my father and his money — only this time you can say them to his face. Then you leave in a fury, and everything's fine. For everybody.'

'Except for him,' she said softly.

'He'll be all right,' Roger assured her. He could do so without reservations. He knew that once the breach had been made, once his father's defences had crumbled, everything would work out. Sam Westwood would soon find himself back to normal; he would shrug off all the unhappiness and disillusionment; freed from his own strange imprisonment, he would step back into his own world. There would be the fast cars and the good restaurants. Sometimes now Roger went into those places where his father had once been known. Business demanded it, and he could cope as confidently as anyone else. But he did not belong. When his father began living again, he would belong. Now the chance was here; the instrument was before him. He said: 'You've got to come in on this. For you there's nothing to lose.'

'I'm aware of that,' she said distantly.

'I've got nothing left.'

'All it means is working hard for a week or two. I'll see you every day. The fact that you won't know our present house or the neighbourhood won't matter at all — Barbara walked out before we moved there. I'll give you enough details of the old place for you to make the right remarks. And I'll drag up every single thing I remember about Barbara herself, as a person. You'll have to sink yourself right into the part so that you think of yourself as Barbara. You'll have to *become* somebody else.'

'Nothing would suit me better' — her voice was dry and somehow very old — 'than to become somebody else.'

5

To become somebody else.

She had tried it so often. In Sollenbury itself she had sought desperately for a new self to believe in — or even a new self to convince other people. Sometimes she seemed to have achieved the latter: certainly she baffled other people, and made them talk about her and stare after her in the street; but inside she was still this unsatisfactory person who never got what she wanted and never gave other people what they wanted. In the end she had come to London . . . and here she was, a Paula Hastings whom Sollenbury might or might not have recognized, but who was all too familiar to herself.

'I don't know who you think *you* are,' her father had so often growled.

She did not know herself.

Her mother and father had never made clear what they expected from her. Sometimes they had made a great fuss of her; at other times her father would let fly in one of his outbursts.

She was the only one of the family who had been to a grammar school. Something working away obscurely in her mother's mind had prompted the resolution that Paula should have a proper schooling. The two older boys had not had it: they had not been encouraged to work at their primary school, and had drifted into the new secondary modern school — 'and none the worse for that,' as Mr. Hastings had growled. Paula was the one they had experimented with. She had had a good teacher at the primary school, and at home she was badgered to do her best. It was like putting a bet on. You took a chance. But naturally you didn't throw away all your money: you just shoved a little bit on, just trying your luck and seeing how it turned up. Paula was nagged into trying hard for the grammar school. She got in, and so had her chance. It was unlikely, from all the signs, that her younger brother and sister would follow her.

'Try anything once,' her father had

sceptically agreed. 'Might as well have one clever 'un in the bunch.'

That was when he was in a good temper. At other times it would be 'that bloody school' and 'airs and graces' and 'bloody books and God knows what'. And inevitably: 'Let me tell you that when I was your age . . . '

Worst of all was her success in the school Dramatic Society. 'Standing up there, makin' a fool of yourself. Play-acting — I never thought to see such nonsense.'

She was deaf to this sort of thing. At last she had found something that mattered. It was not that she wanted others to marvel at her — 'flauntin' yourself, just showin' off, that's what' — but that she loved to lose herself in these ready-made people. She became somebody else. She had a quick ear, and a retentive memory: she reached out and took hold, and captured the essence of other beings. It was intensely satisfying. And there were so few problems. In a play she was complete. She was a neat, self-contained, persuasive person. There was none of the split that was so infuriating in real life — the double realities of home with its noise and derision, and school with its books and the poems and the plays and the music, all leading on to some goal that she was sure she, herself, would never reach. Things had, in a play, been settled in advance: all she had to do was slide into the part and let herself become the person who was there waiting for her. She did not find the restrictions irksome; they comforted her.

It could not last. The refrain became more clamorous: 'Let me tell you that when I was your age . . .'

She had left school when she was fifteen, without even sitting for her general certificate. The headmaster had been annoyed. He had lectured Mr. and Mrs. Hastings on their duties to the child and to the community. Grammar school education could not be given to everyone . . . lucky for those chosen ones who got it . . . full advantage ought to be taken . . . to leave at a crucial moment like this was to throw away all the hard work put in by teachers and by Paula herself.

'There's plenty of hard work for her at home,' Mrs. Hastings had said, glancing at her husband for his support.

Mr. Hastings remained silent. Voluble enough outside about the silliness of the school — 'pack o' fancy smart alecks' — and about how he had managed without that sort of stuff when he was a kid, he sat now with his cap between his knees and sucked the corners of his mouth in, left and right alternately.

The headmaster explained that Paula's being there had kept another child out, and that now her school career had been wasted. Someone else who ought to have had the chance, and who might have benefited from it, was, in effect, deprived of his or her privilege. He shook his head sadly. They were meant to feel guilty.

Mrs. Hastings said stubbornly: 'We've kept her here 's'long as we could. She's had a fair share. But with the younger ones at home, and everything, I can't manage, and that's a fact. She's to come back and do her bit in the house.'

Paula left, and did not greatly regret

leaving. She was at home for two months and then got a job with Madame Cora, the hairdresser. At least her grammar school education had done that much for her: it was a job to be coveted, and the grammar school testimonial helped. 'Can't see what it's got to do with cuttin' hair,' Mr. Hastings grunted. But it helped to be able to say that you had been to that precious school, you couldn't deny that.

Paula was happy enough in the job for a while; and yet not happy. She did not feel that she had been cheated of anything; and yet she was conscious of stirrings of revolt. She had been made different from the rest of her family: her mother and father had deliberately prodded her into being just that bit different, and now they could not expect her to slip back and be exactly the same.

She was aware of an apartness, a sense of being detached from the rest of them. After a while she began to cultivate this sense.

★   ★   ★

'My sister,' said Roger Westwood, 'went to a school at the top of a hill just outside Maidenhead. There was a gravel drive with rhododendrons, and in the spring the crocuses came up through the grass.'

'It sounds . . . nice.'

'It was a dark sort of place. The light never seemed to get into the classrooms, Barbara always said. But it was a good school. Expensive.'

Paula said: 'She'd have learnt things there that I never got a glimmering of. They'd have taught her to talk differently.'

'You talk just as she did. Nothing to worry about there.'

'What were the names of her teachers?'

'The headmistress was a stiff old ramrod of a woman who chain-smoked in her study all day long. Miss Howard, her name was. The girls called her Howie. Then there was Miss Macmillan, who was pretty. They all had a thing about her — except Barbara, who said she couldn't stand that sort of nonsense. Barbara,' he sourly recalled, 'was too much wrapped up in my father. She used to tell us about

67

the way the older girls would hang round Miss Macmillan and write poetry about her. Then Miss Macmillan left. She used to teach in a room painted in brown and dark green, with two Van Gogh reproductions on the walls and an upright piano in the corner.'

'And after that — after leaving the school, where did Barbara go?'

'I'll give you a general outline of that,' said Roger airily. Already he was confident. She was repelled by the brashness of his face and manner, but at the same time fascinated by the whole idea. It was all fantastic yet irresistible. 'It doesn't matter a lot,' he added. 'You can make things up for yourself if you need to, because that was after my father had gone to prison.'

'Well, then; while Barbara was still at home with him . . . '

He put his head on one side with an urchin's cocky grin. 'It's just struck me,' he said: 'you are Barbara. You might as well get used to the idea now.'

She hesitated, then said tentatively: 'When I was still at home, what sort of thing did I used to say to him? How did I speak?'

'Very much as you're speaking now.'

'But — '

'You've got just the right manner,' he said. 'Stiff and sneering — just like Barbara. As though the world was too dirty for you to soil your hands on it.'

★ ★ ★

One year she had been the Sollenbury Beauty Queen, chosen at the August Bank Holiday Carnival. It was the sort of thing the headmaster of the grammar school would have frowned on — he did everything he could to discourage his pupils from entering for such contests — but it was nevertheless a coveted position.

Paula knew that she was the most attractive queen they had had for years. She had been chosen not because she had been a maid of honour for three years and had to be given a turn as beauty queen, and not because she was the daughter of some popular local figure: she had been chosen because she was more beautiful than anyone else in the district.

'A fat lot it means,' growled her father. 'Flauntin' yourself before a lot of gawpin' idiots — that's all there is to it.'

But in some way it lifted her up. She was able to look down on her dull friends, the drab ones who were still at school or leaving for college, talking of becoming school teachers or seeping thankfully into the sooty offices of Sollenbury.

When older women muttered about her in the street, she was pleased.

She married young, and not because she had to, either, no matter what they might say. She married Quentin Gardner, and she was in love with him. Also she liked the idea of becoming Paula Gardner and ceasing to be Paula Hastings.

Quentin was soft-spoken and unlike most of the boys she had met. He was a part-time reporter on the local paper, and they first met when he came to a performance by the Sollenbury Players. Paula had just joined them, being allowed in because of good reports of her school activities: she was not *quite* the sort of person they were used to, but she was young and gifted and useful.

The parts they gave her were not what she would have chosen, but they were parts: for at least a few hours she was engulfed in the otherness of a character in a play. Usually the productions were brittle comedies. Shakespeare and even J. M. Barrie lay behind her. It did not matter greatly. She acquired a new voice, a new manner, a new way of walking and standing, with as much devotion as she had done when her head had been full of resounding lines of verse, when she had strutted in costume and forgotten the men and women in their ordinary clothes out there.

Quentin said she was wasting her time. He always gave the Sollenbury Players a favourable review — it was the done thing — but the first time he took her out he told her exactly what he thought of their general standard and their choice of plays. She was worthy of so many better things — he was sure of it. He talked to her about modern plays, and told her which books to get from the library. He made it clear that he and she understood things that the stunted Sollenbury Players could never comprehend.

Quentin himself was going to do some really important writing one day.

The skin on his shoulders was smoother than she had expected a man's to be, and he had cool hands that she found exciting.

She married him, and grew to hate him.

After he had stayed at home on several consecutive occasions when he ought to have been reporting on local fêtes and bazaars, he was sacked. She went on working while he talked about finding something that would suit him — something that would not prevent his writing that important work that was ready and waiting if he could only get down to it.

She worked until just before the baby was born.

Quentin had a strange talent for staying out of a job and managing to draw National Assistance money without too many questions being asked. Every week he collected the money that they had to live on, and every week she felt herself slipping down — not merely down to the level from which she had so earnestly longed to climb with his help, but into depths she had never envisaged.

Bitterness on her tongue provoked nothing more than gentle reproaches from Quentin.

'But I thought,' he would say, 'you were so different from the others. That's what I saw in you. It's a blow — really it is — to find you're as conventional as all the rest. Money and a safe, stodgy job . . . that's what you've really set your heart on, isn't it? That's what you'd like me to be interested in.'

The baby cried, and he sighed with long-suffering patience. Once he even got out of bed, put on his clothes and went out for a walk, because the noise was upsetting him. Often in the evenings, too, he would go out and leave her in the gas-lit kitchen of their tiny house.

'A nagging wife, eh?' he said lightly, with his most charming grin, when she asked him where he went.

She looked in the glass and saw that she was going to be grey and ugly. Soon;

very soon. A couple of times she took the weekly money he had handed over to her — or, as she thought to herself, the part of it which he had handed over — and went out for a drink, leaving him in with the baby. She had rarely touched spirits before, but she set herself to get drunk and become, even if only briefly, a different person.

She did not succeed. She remained Paula Hastings; not even, in her own mind, Paula Gardner.

There was a night when she went out and came back late, and Quentin was not in. Michael was crying upstairs — crying with a hoarse, hysterical sobbing that told he had been alone for a long time.

It happened again, soon afterwards. This time a neighbour heard it. A complaint was made, and added to other things. Paula, outraged, was visited by a girl slightly older than herself, dressed in a trim, cheap grey suit, who intimated that there was a possibility of the child being taken out of the custody of its parents . . . of proceedings . . . of solemn, high-minded action . . .

She had her first open row with Quentin. He was hurt. Before long she had another. He was still hurt, but showed that he was capable of hurting back. Their life took on a new colour, a new pattern. They quarrelled, and after each quarrel there was no reconciliation. She discovered that Quentin's smooth tongue could become harsh; she was scoured by his vindictiveness.

And more clearly than ever, in spite of all she had done and all she had longed to do, she was Paula Hastings. Yet no longer Hastings — she had never really belonged to her family, and now was quite cut off from them: she was simply Paula, as she had always been.

Now that she and Quentin were open enemies, sharpening claws and blunting words on one another, they set up strangely puritanical standards. If she went out in the evening, she knew that Quentin would not himself slink out later and leave Michael in the house alone: after their near-humiliation at the hands of the authorities, that would be against his principles. There were certain absolutes which they both accepted;

certain rules which neither would break, but which each hoped to torment or lure the other into breaking.

A long time went by before she came home and again found that he was not there. But he had not left Michael: he had taken Michael with him.

The truth did not resolve itself from her frenzy and then from her despair until late the following day. Quentin had gone to see one of his women — one of the sympathetic young women who believed, as Paula had once done, that he would soon write something important and be among those who created splendour and made money without having to strive too hard, too long. He had stuck to his new principles. Rather than leave Michael in the house alone, he had taken the child with him. What the two of them did with Michael for an hour or two was never decided: it was a question that no one wished to pursue, and that could add nothing to the final result anyway. What was certain was that Michael travelled in the back of the young woman's small car on the way home, and that he did not reach home. It was mentioned that, being in the back seat, he did not have as much glass in him as the other two had.

The young woman had been Sollenbury Beauty Queen two years after Paula.

★ ★ ★

Roger Westwood said: 'You used to call him Sammy. Remember that.'

'But would I go back to it right away? After what I've said about him . . . '

He looked at her with dawning respect. 'That's quite a point. You're dead right. Come to think of it, that makes it all the better. You don't have to worry about being stiff and nervous when you first meet him. That's O.K. Take your time. Let him break down your resistance. Say two weeks — three weeks at most. Unless it works out so that you feel it's all right to get going faster. But when he's good and ready, and you know the time has come — well, you call him Sammy. Get it?'

'I'll remember,' she said.

They were sitting in his room behind

77

Marylebone Road. She had been doubtful about coming here, at first — doubtful yet resigned. Now, as the lesson proceeded, she accepted what she had glimpsed at the start: she saw that he was truly single-minded, and that his father's money was all that he wanted. No, not quite that: his father's money was the symbol of his father's power, and he wanted a share in both. There was no time for anything else.

Almost she began to like him, or at least to admire him. The intensity of his application, and the lengths to which he was prepared to go, awoke an echo in her. Roger Westwood did not intend to remain the same, incomplete Roger Westwood all his life. He thought that he knew of a way out, and he proposed to try it.

'Your hair style,' he said.

'What about it?'

'You'll have to alter it. Barbara had the same colour hair as yours — same texture, I'd say — but she always had it pulled back behind her ears.'

'You mean,' she said, 'that that's how she did it when your father knew her? But she must have changed it in all sorts of ways later.'

'Never. It was always the same.'

'It's hard to imagine. Most girls . . . women . . . well, it's queer.'

He said: 'Barbara was . . . I mean, *you* . . . were queer. Stiff and awkward and sure of yourself. Always.'

He got up and crossed the room to a chest of drawers wedged into the corner. One of the drawers squealed as he pulled it open.

It was not an expensive room. There was a modern cocktail cabinet against one wall, but the wallpaper behind it was scarred and faded. The shade on the lamp had been bought recently, somewhere fashionable, but the flex dropped slackly down the wall from an old point. The carpet was meant to cover the entire floor but curled away from the corners, and the door of the built-in cupboard beside her chair did not fit. She saw the signs of his tastes, his forward-groping desires — the television set, the bottles in the cocktail cabinet, the American magazines lying on the small Swedish table — but she saw also that he had a long way to go.

She said: 'Suppose she were to come back in the middle of it all, just when I was going strong?'

Roger straightened up and closed the drawer. He laughed incredulously. 'You think of the most wonderful things, don't you?'

'But suppose she did?'

He sat down again, this time on the edge of his chair. He held out a bundle of snapshots to her, and one postcard-size enlargement.

There was a picture of a child of three or four years of age on a seaside promenade, holding her father's hand. Then, a few years older, she had her arm linked with his. The enlargement showed the head and shoulders of a girl in her middle teens, with pursed, sardonic lips and eyes that stared beyond the camera rather than at it. Paula recognized the face and yet knew that it was unfamiliar: she might have been looking into a distorting mirror.

Other snapshots showed the whole family, with Roger often hanging slightly back or turning his head archly away.

Barbara always stared arrogantly ahead, but never right into the camera.

Roger said: 'You can see what sort of girl she was, can't you?'

'Sure of herself,' murmured Paula. It was not envy that she felt: she did not wish to be this girl; yet she would have liked to experience for herself that assurance of rightness.

'And having walked out,' said Roger, 'she'll stay out.'

'Perhaps you're right.'

'I've got to be right.'

Absently she went through the snapshots, then turned them over and started at the beginning again. She was imbibing an atmosphere. With the evidence before her she was trying to re-create a family. These black and white images had once been alive, and to draw close to them today she must know their yesterdays.

She bent over a faded scene in which Sam Westwood stood with one hand on the door-handle of his Bentley.

Quietly Roger said: 'Barbara.'

She did not lift her head.

Again he said: 'Barbara.'

This time she responded. 'Oh . . . yes. Sorry.'

'You'll have to be quicker than that.'

'I know. I'm sorry.'

'We've only got tomorrow.' She heard the trembling excitement in his voice. 'Then we drive down.'

She caught her breath. The monstrous impossibility of the whole situation suddenly weighed down on her. It was still not too late to turn back, was it?

He sensed nothing. Already he was living in tomorrow, and the day after. He said: 'One more session, and then I can show him . . . what I've found.'

⋆　⋆　⋆

Had she ever truly been found, by anyone?

Fleeing from Sollenbury, she had been sure that Paula was dead. As dead as her husband and her child. More than that, even: there had never been any such person. Paula had not existed, and so her son could not have existed. There had never been a Michael. It was impossible that he should have chuckled in the way that she remembered — no, not remembered, but dreamed — and then been not there. The only solution must be that he had never been there.

Reaching London, she would discover herself or be discovered. It was time she acquired a self that she and others would recognize.

And she must be happy. There were ways of being happy. Misery was something that you left behind with your cast-off skin in Sollenbury.

She went to theatres and to casting offices. She grew used to the shaken heads, the tired shrugs. Experience . . . ? She grew used, also, to the suppressed laughter. In the mirror of men's eyes she saw something, but it was never what she was looking for.

In due course she reached the office where Stan Morrison said to her: 'Acting? This isn't a film magazine company, honey. But my father runs some smart clubs — plenty of big names have started there — I might have a word with him about you. Later. Right now we could use you as a pin-up girl. Why not? A lot of the stars began as pin-up girls. Why not . . . '

They paid her well. It amused her to see the copies of these magazines lying on bookstalls and in the corners of poky shops and on barrows or shelves at the bottom of streets under the metallic roar of a railway bridge; to turn over the pages and see herself, and to know how well she had been paid for sitting or lying in that studio, with the strips of material tied round her.

It was puzzling, though, to see how slack and sad were the faces of the men who peered at the magazines and, fumbling for money, hastily bought copies. For a few weeks she exulted in her body and the knowledge of its power; but when she saw the shamefaced men and was aware of their sadness, the exultation faded.

Later she wore nothing, and by now she was curious rather than hopeful. Looking at a glossy print, looking at a page in a magazine, she studied the face and breasts and legs of a complete stranger, and said over and over to herself: 'That is Paula Hastings.'

Still it was nobody she knew.

Perhaps it did not matter. She was alive. There was plenty of time. She ate and drank and slept, and went out with one of the other girls who was often at the studio, until the other girl turned down the chance of an increased rate of pay.

'If they think I'm going to go in for that sort of thing . . . '

Paula did not turn it down. She was outside this flesh and bone, unconvinced by it and undisturbed by its physical humiliations. The lights burned, the cameras stared at her; somewhere the printing presses duplicated and reduplicated her; and she was paid.

The cameras did not discover who she was. They revealed so much to greedy, sad-eyed men turning over pages, but to Paula they revealed nothing.

It was a dull, routine, respectable world, this world of the studio.

She moved from it into the world of Lew Morrison.

'I've spoken to my father about you.' It was Stan Morrison who said it, leaning in the door of his office and pointing a cigarette at her. 'He'd like to see you. Might be a good opening for you.'

Hope was as wavering as a candle flame. She was not prepared to let herself expect too much.

Stan Morrison said: 'Don't think you're going to be a star overnight. Just take what comes, and play your cards right, and the old man'll treat you fine. I can promise you that.'

It would be a beginning. She met Lew Morrison, and knew that it would be impossible to be a nobody in his hectic world. Lew Morrison, with his veiled eyes and half-insulting questions, would not be interested in a nobody. Here she might find the person who had been lying in wait within herself.

This time she was right. This time she found Paula Hastings — that same Paula she had left behind, for ever, in Sollenbury.

It had been easy to let herself drift from one stage to another, from the first photographic poses to the next, from the studio to Lew Morrison's club. Easy to say that it didn't matter; that you would get used to anything; that nobody could, really, touch you. Easy to sneer at the faint stirrings of the provincial girl buried so deeply inside you. A hard, confident smile would carry you through; a shrug of indifference showed how little you really cared . . .

Until the bright, brittle world narrowed and closed in. Until other people receded into the background and you knew that you had been marked down by one of Lew Morrison's clients — this man with a thick lower lip and moist, cold hands, that man with the face of a film star and the persistent high giggle of a maniac, or the fat little dwarf with slanting eyes.

She discovered Paula Hastings. It was the old, inescapable Paula Hastings who sobbed and was sick. It was a frightened, nauseated child who clawed a man's face and fled — and it was the older, wiser Paula without hope and without illusion who told Lew Morrison that she was leaving and why, and what she thought of him.

In reply he told her what the future of a girl such as herself was likely to be. He also told her how powerful he was, and promised her with cold intensity that, in the world in which she would have to live from now on, there would be no place for her. He would make sure of that. Women didn't let Lew Morrison and his friends down like this.

'I can get an ordinary job,' she said.

'You can't,' he said. 'Not now. You wouldn't settle. You're not the sort. I know. Believe me, I know.'

Yes, he knew.

★　★　★

The flow of traffic had thinned some miles back. They were driving now through a stretch of sparse woodland, with a few dry leaves still blowing across the road.

She was acutely conscious of every feature of the countryside. Her eyes were tired: she had been unable to withdraw her attention, to relax in the car and conserve her energies for the meeting that was now so close. She read road signs and signposts, advertisements, the names on shops; and now her head turned compulsively to watch the trees flickering past, as dizzying as the march of telegraph poles seen from a train.

Roger said: 'There's nothing to be worried about. This is going to work beautifully.' The knuckles of his hand on the wheel were white. 'If you get stuck at any time at all, just play it steady. Keep calm. Don't say a thing. He'll expect you to be moody and unsettled, and you can be as dumb as you want to when it suits you.'

'Are we nearly there?' she said.

'And when it comes to getting the details about the Mannerlaw stuff out of him . . .'

They slowed for a sharp turn. A signpost rose from a green triangle of grass. Paula looked at it and read its fatal message. She sat as stiff and unyielding as though they might at any moment crash; almost she wished that they would.

'Look down your nose at the whole business,' Roger was saying. 'That's what Barbara would have done. I mean, that's what *you* would always do. When you get round to talking about it, make it quite casual. Say you can't imagine why he — how would you put it? — oh, yes ... you simply can't imagine why he's making such a *thing* of it. Laugh a bit, and shake your head. Then talk about something else. And later, begin to wheedle it out of him, only all the time you've got to look as though you didn't give a damn.'

She hardly heard what he was saying. He went on: he could not stop talking. He was like a nervous producer harassing an actor at the last moment, just as the curtain was about to rise.

Which, really, was what he was.

She saw the water below them. Cold sunshine touched wavetips and scored a faint steely line along the horizon.

Roger broke off, and suddenly, quietly, said: 'Barbara.'

'Yes?' she responded, without looking away from the unfolding coastline.

'That's good,' he approved. 'That was fine.'

They ran parallel with the sea, and now the house was there ahead of them, waiting for them.

6

Mrs. Westwood must have been well primed by her son. As the car drew up she opened the front door of the house and stood there with one hand to her breast in a histrionic gesture.

Roger got out and came round the car impatiently to open the door for Paula.

She said: 'Did you normally behave so politely to your sister?'

He stopped. 'That's a thought.'

She got out.

The woman on the doorstep raised her arms as though to draw Paula towards her. She was a large, heavy woman who ought to have looked imposing yet failed to be so. There was a faded magnificence about her — slightly drooping shoulders where there should have been confidence, lines of worry and disillusion where there should have been plump self-assurance.

Suddenly she moved aside. A man came and stood in the opening. He stared. Paula began to walk towards him.

She could almost feel Roger coming up behind her, treading silently as though not to distract attention from the leading player. The man in the doorway did not take his eyes off her face.

Somebody had to speak.

It was Mrs. Westwood who ran clumsily forward and threw her arms around Paula.

'You've come back,' she cried. 'Barbara, you've come back.'

It was loud and unreal. She was, or had been, a statuesque woman, and this supposedly impulsive run was out of character. Seen close to, her face was stained with blobs of a strange red flush.

She turned, with one arm still around Paula, and faced her husband.

He whispered: 'Hello . . . Barbara.'

'Hello,' she said. Then she added: 'Father.'

His gaze seemed to plunge right into her — a remorseless light fingering into dark corners.

'Well,' said Roger. 'Well. Shall we all go inside and celebrate?'

They went indoors, Paula jostled by Mrs. Westwood, heavy against her. Sam Westwood — 'Father,' she said insistently to herself — was behind her. As they went into a room at the back of the house he moved up beside her.

He was not deceived. He must know that she was not his daughter. She wondered when he would speak, and how he would decide to attack her.

'Now, Sam, give them both a drink while I get lunch on the table,' Mrs. Westwood fussed, prodding Paula towards a chair and giving her a speculative glance as she did so. 'Won't be long. Good job I've got plenty of things in. Of course, if I'd known' — she flashed a twisted, surreptitious smile at Roger — 'I'd have had something special. But I couldn't have known, could I?'

Sam went to the cupboard near the window. He bent down, opened it, and then turned round.

'You'll . . . have a drink? You drink nowadays?'

Paula laughed sharply. 'Yes. I'm a big girl now.'

It was the right thing to say: Roger, at any rate, thought so, and nodded at her across his father's bent back.

'Of course,' said Sam Westwood in a small voice. 'It's just one of the things that's happened, isn't it? It'll take some getting used to.'

He was such a cowed, deflated man that she felt a surge of contempt — not for him, but for Roger and herself. Or, rather, for Barbara. Had Barbara, even as a child, spoken to him like this? Had he allowed it, and still loved her? And if not — if Barbara's sourness had come only later — why did she have to ape the later Barbara; why not be gentle and sympathetic, as perhaps he remembered her, and coax the truth out of him that way?

He was asking her a question. She looked blankly at him and then said: 'Oh, sorry. Dubonnet, please.'

'Just Dubonnet?'

'Please.'

He was a stranger. Even if she had been the true Barbara, he would have been a stranger. Politely he was handing her a glass; politely they were nodding and

94

drinking; politely she looked out of the window and made the sort of remark that a visitor would make:

'You're very isolated here.'

'Yes, aren't we?' Then he looked puzzled. 'But haven't you — '

'Barbara,' said Roger smoothly, 'never came down here at all. It's quite new to her.'

Sam Westwood at last averted his eyes.

'It must be deadly in the winter,' said Paula, with a harsh brusqueness that surprised even herself.

'We don't know that yet,' said Sam. Quickly he went on, with the urgency of a still unexpressed fear that she might not be staying: 'Once we've settled in it'll be ideal. A nice warm fire — the town's not so far away — lovely walking on fine crisp days round here. You see. You wait and see.'

He lifted his head again, and the appeal was naked in his face. She saw that she had been wrong. He did not suspect her yet. And however undemonstrative he might be, the awareness of her presence was sinking into him. It was beginning to mean more to him, minute by minute. Paula felt a flicker of inexplicable alarm.

Mrs. Westwood came in.

'That can wait for a little while now. Won't be long.'

She had changed into a dress that had been expensive when it was new. It was incongruous against the bareness of the land outside. But it showed that she had once been a beautiful woman and that she had had the right clothes for her type. This dark blue dress had a richness that emphasized her rather florid complexion; and it had an immediately perceptible influence on the way she spoke. The breathlessness of her manner just after Paula's arrival had changed. She sat down with a languid smile, took a glass of sherry from her husband with a deliberately slow movement, and leaned back with a very gentle, very self-assured little sigh.

'Now, darling,' she said in a voice that Paula sensed belonged to her past, 'tell us what you have been doing with yourself.'

It sounded playful. But it was all calculated. Roger had probably rehearsed this as he had rehearsed so many other possible lines with Paula. She knew what to say: she took her cue and answered Mrs. Westwood. Both of them were really talking to Sam Westwood.

The story had all been worked out in detail. She told them, in naturally brief spasms, about the job she had taken in a good dress shop. She described her room in Hampstead, casually, lingering on it for just long enough to emphasize a slight note of regret — as though the casualness were a veil for her real feelings.

'Leave it in the air,' Roger had instructed her. 'Make out that you were having a pretty good time, and you're perfectly capable of going back there. The least little thing — any attempt to cross you in anything — and you can walk out. Keep him worrying.'

She knew that she was succeeding in this. Sam Westwood was worrying, all right.

He said hardly a word then or at lunch. Roger and Mrs. Westwood steered the conversation into the agreed channels. Paula answered their questions, occasionally glancing at Sam as though to draw him in; and every now and then, as planned, there was a silence. The silence, like the implications behind all her words, was meant to worry him.

All the time he watched her. He had nothing to say to her, yet he could not tear his gaze away from her. She shivered. All at once she thought of the men who had pawed magazines on bookstalls, bought them and fingered through them at home, brooded over the frozen, captured lines of her body. The greed in his eyes was nearly the same.

What would they say to one another when they were alone together?

'We're settling in very nicely,' Mrs. Westwood was saying across the table. 'You never thought we would, dear, did you?'

Roger looked at her.

'No,' she said curtly, 'I certainly didn't.'

'It just shows you — '

'What does it show?' she snapped. This was the part as she had been schooled in it; this was how Roger had built up Barbara for her; yet it did not ring true. Or perhaps she was quite the wrong person for the role.

Mrs. Westwood said: 'Your father was quite right. This is just the right sort of place. Here we can . . . well, get used to one another again.'

She turned to smile at her husband. It was a practised smile, but somehow one felt that it had not been used for a long time. It did not belong with the finely etched lines on her cheeks and in the corners of her mouth.

Sam Westwood cleared his throat. His wife remained for a second with the vegetable dish poised in her hands, then lowered it gently to the table.

He said: 'You've given up your job, then?'

'Yes,' she said. She paused. 'For the time being, anyway.'

Every word seemed painful. 'You're going to stay here?' His voice crackled with the dryness in his throat.

'I'll look around,' she said lightly. 'There might be an amusing job in — what's the name of the place along the sea front?'

'Easterdyke,' said Roger.

His father said: 'There's no question of getting a job. You don't have to. As long as you want to stay here, you stay here.'

'We're rich?' she said sceptically.

The silence was unbearable. Roger and his mother were too tense. Surely the man could see; surely he must know what they were up to?

'Just don't worry about it,' he said. 'I'm telling you that you can stay here. If you want any money, tell me.'

She was half tempted to ask now, to come right out and lead him on to telling her where the diamonds had been hidden. It was a natural opening; it would be perfectly natural for her to flash some derisive, snappish question at him. The sooner it was over, the better. The sooner the question was asked and answered, the sooner she could get away. And she was very anxious to get away.

But she could not do it. Not yet. His own slow speech and the slowness of his reactions imposed their tempo on her.

'I'll see how things go,' she heard her own voice saying. She was detached from it, as she was detached from the other

100

people in this room.

She looked round at them. Roger and his mother and father . . . they did not seem to belong together any more than she, for her part, belonged to them. She had an odd feeling that she was not the only fraud in the room. They were all playing parts, and not one of them was convincing. Four strangers, each wanting something, but not wanting it for any of the others; not loving . . . not living.

Roger began: 'Of course, the trouble with Babs . . . '

She was glad that he was talking. In this moment of detachment she felt that the part she had been chosen to play was falling to pieces in her hands. If she had been forced to speak, she would have given the game away: she would have said something wildly out of character. Now she could sit back and let the others play out their scene.

What did they want, each of them? Roger wanted money and power, that was all. Perhaps, somewhere, he also wanted his father's affection — or, at least, respect; but it was all bound up with the money and the person his father had once been, not what he was now. Mrs. Westwood presumably wanted things to be as they had once been. Her demands were few but expensive. The cost of surface respectability on a certain social level was high. Paula knew these things — had learnt them without experiencing them, in the confused world she had so recently left. She saw Mrs. Westwood only as a surface: such complications as there were must be simple, commonplace.

And Sam Westwood . . . ?

All she knew of his desires was his longing to have his daughter back.

The thought of it drew her inexorably back into the company of the three Westwoods. She could no longer stand aloof. They reclaimed her as they got up from the table, and Roger turned towards her with a vague remark that was of no consequence but had to be acknowledged.

'That was better than some of these office snacks I've been having lately,' she said stiffly.

Her mother — for a second she actually visualized Mrs. Westwood as her mother, before she again became a stranger — coloured, and Paula knew that the compliment had been out of character. But what was so wrong with it? She had had to say something: she could not use only the set lines they had planned. Conversation went on, day after day, and its twists and turns could not be foreseen. She was bound to make mistakes; bound to fumble a remark or two as she tried to fill in a gap.

She began to stack plates and move towards the kitchen.

Mrs. Westwood said: 'Go and sit down and . . . talk to your father. Roger can clear the table today, for once.'

'Sure,' said Roger. 'Go along, you two.'

'No, I — '

'Do as you're told,' murmured Sam Westwood with a tight flicker of a smile. 'Mustn't argue with your mother, my girl.'

She did not want to be alone with him. But the other two were deserting her. She followed her quarry, her selected victim ('Father,' she firmly said in her mind), into the sitting-room.

A few steps inside the door, he turned. She stood before him. He said:

'I'm glad you came back, Barbie. So glad. I . . . I've been waiting for you for so long.'

She put out one hand and touched his arm, and moved closer. He threw his arms round her and hugged her. If she had been a little girl — the little girl he remembered and was, in his heart, hugging now — he would have lifted her off her feet and swung her round.

She found words. 'I'm glad too,' she managed. 'I'm glad . . . Sammy.'

When he released her she was trembling with fear. The plan was working. There had been no slip yet; no suspicion. He accepted her as Barbara. And his belief was somehow far more terrifying than disbelief could have been. She *was* Barbara: she was trapped.

7

They had walked in an unbroken but companionable silence along the sea wall from the house to Easterdyke. On the outskirts of the small town, Sam Westwood had turned inland, and on the slope of a hill they approached an old pub. It seemed to have been made of several bits and pieces of other buildings: there were three different roof levels, and the walls all sagged slightly outwards.

'Nice old place. Very soothing.' It was the first thing Sam had said for thirty minutes.

This was her third day. Unconsciously she was relaxing. She had enjoyed this brisk walk in the cold October morning. It would have been easy to believe that she was on a holiday — a late holiday in crisp, windy weather by the exhilaratingly restless sea.

Being alone with Sam Westwood was not the ordeal she had expected it to be.

Actually they were not on their own very much: she was beginning to realize that he, too, was nervous. He was not yet ready to be with her when there were no other people around. He treated her as though she were fragile and might easily break. His shyness was endearing. Once she had grasped the fact that he was being so careful not to 'rush' her — that he dreaded the thought of driving her away and was not going to say too much until he was sure of their relationship — she found herself fitting in unobtrusively with his mood. It suited her. Soon she would have to act. Soon she must get down to the distasteful job for which she had been engaged. But not immediately. 'Take it easy,' Roger had said before he went back to London for a few days. 'Don't force the pace. Try to judge the right moment for it.' She was glad to find excuses for postponing the decision of what constituted the right moment.

The trees on the hillside broke the wind. The two of them stopped and turned to look back at the landscape below.

'There's the house,' said Sam, 'over there.'

'Yes.' From here it was tiny and insignificant. When the wind blew like this, and the saltings were so clearly etched over such a great distance, all human affairs seemed insignificant. It was only when you were indoors, enclosed, that you felt the oppression of other people and other people's problems.

He tucked her arm into his, unthinkingly. It was not a demonstrative gesture: it happened, and she accepted it, and the two of them were friends.

He said: 'On a day like this you can see every boat in Easterdyke Harbour.'

'You can nearly read the numbers on their sides,' she agreed.

'And count the feathers on the birds in the creek.'

'And the blades of grass — '

'And the sands on the shore.'

They laughed absurdly. With his free hand he began to point out places he had been to in the last few weeks. He sketched in for her a small universe. It was the engrossing universe of a man who had nothing in common with the man Roger had described to her. She wondered whether to write to Roger, or to telephone him — to tell him that he had made a mistake, and might as well give up, for this man was a peace-lover, a stroller and a quietist, a man who wished simply to stand and stare.

Then she dismissed the thought. She did not want, here and now, even to think of Roger and their plans. Just being here, on a day like this, was enough.

Abruptly he said: 'We never went to the seaside much, did we?'

He had taken her unawares. Panic seized her. This could be a catch-question. She turned her face away, baffled. Of course it could not be a trick question: she could not have been that mistaken about his mood; but it did not help, for she still did not know the answer.

A simple one. All she could say was: 'No. No, I suppose we didn't.'

'Do you like it better nowadays?'

The answer came as suddenly as his question had done. Roger's lessons had included this. She had hated swimming — had made appalling scenes at her school when swimming lessons threatened. Tiny, she had turned her back on the sea and grimly made sand castles, merely to keep herself occupied and be able to ignore the vastness of the water.

She said: 'I think I could probably be persuaded to paddle — when the summer comes.'

His flush of happiness robbed the morning of its clear contentment. She felt guilty, seeing what she had done. *When the summer comes . . . .* She had told him that she would be staying.

'And over there,' he said, pointing, and smiling, 'the heronry. Next year — '

'Brrr.' She shivered artificially.

'Cold?' At once he was moving, as she had meant him to do, towards the door of the old inn. 'Let's go and see what we can get.'

The interior was chill but welcoming. Logs burned in a huge open fireplace, throwing out little heat until one was within a few feet of it. The ceiling was low, supported by gnarled beams. It all looked old and traditional, but a radio was muttering away in a back room, and there was a calendar on the wall featuring a girl dressed in black net stockings and a cluster of feathers. Paula glanced at it and glanced away again: it was too familiar, too reminiscent.

When Sam Westwood brought her a drink, and they stood close to the fire, she was conscious of the walls closing in again. To come in here had seemed, on the spur of the moment, an escape. Now she was not so sure. In a restricted space like this he became too real. He was not just a figure in a plan, as he had been when she and Roger had talked about him; and he was not the undemanding companion with whom she had walked here through the morning's brightness.

'A penny for them,' he said.

The relays in her mind clicked, and the response was easy: 'Worth umpteen pounds.'

Again it meant a lot to him. These echoes were, perhaps, what he had lived on for so many years.

'Umpteen pounds, then.'

'Actually,' she said, 'I don't know that I was thinking about anything special.'

'I refuse to pay up, then.'

Was this the moment? Talk of payment struck a note that could be taken up: the theme could swiftly develop.

But she only said: 'It's such a nice morning.'

Sam looked round the bar. There were only three others in it at this time of the morning, and they were three elderly men who sat round a table in the corner, their heads nodding inwards, utterly absorbed.

He took a deep breath. 'You like it here? You're not thinking of going away again?'

'I haven't had much time to consider it. Yet.'

'I hope you won't.'

'Well . . . ' She had to force herself to say it: 'It all depends.'

'On what?'

'It's too soon to say.'

His whisper seemed overpoweringly loud. To her ears it seemed to resound through the bar. 'But you're thinking about it — I can tell. Don't you enjoy

111

coming out with me like this? I suppose I'm . . . pretty dull.' Apology changed to attack. 'Why did you go away in the first place, Barbie?'

'I needed time to think.'

'That's not what you told Roger.'

'Roger had no business to . . . oh, I suppose he had. I didn't mean to come back. I imagine he told you that, too.'

'He did. But you came back.'

'It was so stupid, really.' She put her empty glass down on a black oak table near the fireplace. 'There wasn't any point in making a great flourish about it.'

'Wasn't there?'

'Looking back at it now — '

'Never mind about looking back at it.' She sensed now what his anger, controlled yet savage, must have been when he was a big, healthy man. 'What I'm getting at is what your feelings were like when you . . . when you decided you couldn't bear to meet me again.'

On this there should be no difficulty. She had worked this out thoroughly with Roger. But she did not let her own, contrived anger loose. She stooped over the table and let time run through her fingers as, very slowly, she picked up her glass and turned, holding it out.

'Do you think I could have another one, Sammy?'

She watched his back as he went to the counter. Sammy. His wife, she had been told, had never called him that. It was Barbara's name for him, and it had been understood that nobody else could use it.

She wondered about them. What was existence like for the two of them now? She tried to imagine them before she came — the two of them, with Barbara gone and Roger working in London for the larger part of the time. How had they talked, what pattern of life together had they been able to establish; what did they mean to one another?

He came back with the glasses. He might have been reading her mind. Without preamble, he said:

'I suppose you think it's a queer set-up, the way I . . . wander about on my own?'

'You're not on your own today.'

'But I don't bring your mother,' he said. 'I haven't done, at all. We haven't gone out together since I got back.'

'Have you asked her to come with you?'

'Not once,' he said.

'She's not happy.' They were treading on uncertain ground.

'You think I'm not being fair to her?'

'I think,' she plunged, 'that she . . . that Mother wants things. You ought to do something to settle her mind. All our minds,' she added with an impatient jerk of her head.

He was deaf to her meaning. Abstractedly he said: 'The trouble is, I'm not human any longer. You stop being human when you've been in prison for a few years. It's hard to explain, but it happens. Either you harden — they're the lucky ones, maybe — and you come out determined to get your own back on the whole system that put you there; or else you cease to live. I ceased.'

'It's not true,' she said. 'And it's not fair on the others — the people you've left outside, waiting for you.'

'There isn't such a place as outside. You are inside, and there are people on top of you and crowded all around you. Even when there's silence, it's thick and heavy. When I came out I . . . I didn't want to talk. I still don't. To anyone but you.'

She said: 'Sammy — '

'All you want when you're free . . . Free,' he mused, sidetracked by a word. 'This is what they call being free. But I don't feel that I've got away. Somehow I almost lost my voice while I was inside — and I lost more than that. Whatever it is that you've lost, you don't find it again when you get out. All you want is peace. No, not just peace: nullity. You don't want to exist, so you will yourself to stop existing.'

'I know,' she said.

Now he smiled, faintly. 'You couldn't know,' he said, touching her arm.

But I know, she said to herself.

Footsteps creaked on wooden stairs within the wall at their backs. A door opened, and a tall young man with sandy hair came into the bar.

Sam Westwood swung towards him, greeting him with relief.

'Hello, Adam. Wondered if we'd see you this morning.'

'It'd be an odd morning when you didn't.'

The young man glanced at Sam's glass, took a step towards the counter, and then became aware of Paula. He stopped.

Sam said: 'I'd like you to meet my daughter. Barbara, this is Adam Collier — he has the good fortune to be living in this establishment.'

His hand was strong and supple. She looked into a pair of startling blue eyes, full of laughter and shrewdness. Her first thought was that he ran a grave risk of banging his head on the beams.

'Sam's told me about you,' he said.

'Not a lot.' Sam's quick, sibilant assurance was meant to put her at her ease.

'By no means a lot,' Adam Collier agreed. 'Not nearly enough, in fact. He didn't even mention that you were expected home from the big city this week.'

'It was a last-minute decision,' she said.

'I'm glad it was made.'

Perhaps his smile was too frank, his charm too ready; but certainly his arrival had brought life into the room. He was commandingly taking Sam's glass from him, and cocking an enquiring eyebrow at her own. A few seconds later they were sitting at one of the tables, and two new arrivals had started a sociable buzz of conversation in one of the other corners.

'Adam,' said her father — and with the introduction of a total stranger he became in some disconcerting way more solidly her father — 'is a writer. Or so he says. I think it's only an excuse.' He grinned. He was happier than she had seen him. This was a friend: it was a man's relationship, making no personal demands. 'Writers can work when and where they like — and you can always say that you stay at a country pub in order to get local colour.'

'Nevertheless,' returned Adam easily, 'I write.'

Paula asked: 'What sort of thing?'

'My present opus' — he gave his shoulders an engagingly self-conscious wriggle — 'is a rather dull little thing about economics and our present society.'

'And you need to stay in the country to write that?'

Sam chuckled. It was a refreshing

sound. 'I wondered about that, too. I thought economics were worked out in the cities these days, not on the land.'

'You can see 'em more clearly from a distance,' said Adam Collier.

They were talking about nothing. He did not look like a writer — but perhaps writers never did — and she could not believe that Sam cared about writers and writing anyway; but somehow the conversation took wing, and they were all three laughing, and there was a clink as glasses were gathered together and taken to the bar, and more laughter.

She knew that Adam Collier was studying her from time to time. His expression was something she was used to: she had experienced it before. But there was an undertone that was new. He liked her being there, and he was a man who liked women — but also he was puzzled. Or at any rate curious in a probing, analytical sort of way.

'Shall we be seeing a lot of you down here now?' he asked.

'It all depends.' It was the best answer. At so many times, in so many places, it had been the best answer.

'Let's hope she stays,' said Adam to Sam.

'Here's hoping,' said Sam — not yet confidently, but with an infectious cheerfulness that she had not encountered in him before.

He was not drunk. He was not even slightly irresponsible. It was just that for the first time he was relaxed, and what must have been the old Sam Westwood was reasserting himself.

Adam sprawled his long legs across the fireplace.

Paula said: 'It must be nice, to work where you want to work, when you feel like it.'

He wrinkled up his eyes thoughtfully. She had seen a picture like that, once — it came back to her confusingly, then resolved itself: it had been the picture of a young, grinning fox cub, adorable yet lean and savage.

'Things can go wrong,' he said into his glass. 'Things don't always work out the way you expect — or the way you want them to.'

'No,' said Sam with a solemn shake of his head.

Paula laughed. 'Sammy — '

'What's the matter?'

'The two of you. You look so philosophical. Or something.'

'Or something,' Adam repeated.

She was suddenly uncomfortable. She wanted to leave. And yet at the same time she did not want to break away from this warm, cosy circle. Everything was false and wrong, and the moments of instinctive, natural pleasure were only spasmodic — and then they, too, were wrong because they clashed with reality. She ought not to be sitting and talking. She ought to be neither enjoying nor hating the company of Adam Collier and Sam Westwood: her job was to be cool and calculating, to concentrate on working out the best means and the right moment for asking Sam Westwood where he had hidden a fortune.

She still smiled, and turned towards Adam as he spoke. But she was thinking: It's time we got away from here, it's too comfortable and too uncomfortable.

Sam Westwood said: 'It's time we got away from here. It's too comfortable — our healthy outdoor programme is being undermined, eh, Barbie?'

His opening words and his whole inflection were so much the same as what she had heard in her mind that she was at a loss to reply. He had taken her up as swiftly as an echo. There was a twinkle of complicity in his eyes as though he understood just what she had been thinking. Which was absurd. But the sensation of swift, tingling contact remained.

Earlier this morning he had picked up, as he might have snatched it from the air, her speculations about himself and his wife. Now this. It was true, then, what Roger had said: there had always been this close bond between Sam Westwood and his daughter, and . . .

But it was nonsense! *She* was not Barbara Westwood. For a fantastic moment she had felt the kinship, believed that it existed between this father and this daughter.

He was not her father. She was not his daughter.

'Time we weren't here,' said Sam.

Adam Collier was lurching to his feet and smiling down at them. His heartiness seemed too good to be true, yet she was disturbed and unsure of herself when he said: 'We'll meet again, won't we? We've just got to meet again.'

★   ★   ★

There was a telephone in the inn, but he used it only to answer incoming calls — and there had so far been only two of those. For his own calls he waited until he was in Easterdyke itself, in the impersonal telephone-box with the background music, even through the closed door, of the same gnawing at the shingle.

'Hello, Fred. No, you can scrub that out. I'm not coming back. Something new. Yes, new . . . No, I'm not wasting my time. Not any longer. At least, I don't think so . . . The daughter's arrived. Yes, the daughter. The one we got all that detail on. It looks as though she's come home to get the old man's secrets out of him. I've a hunch something is going to break — I can feel it in the air.'

A bus rumbled past; the sea pounded its cymbals; the voice on the line was metallic and matter-of-fact.

'Of course,' Adam replied. 'You know me. I'll turn on the charm. Yes, all of it. I don't often get the chance of doing it and getting paid for it, do I? Leave it to me. I'm fairly confident now.'

He rang off and left the telephone-box. The wind off the sea snatched at his breath. It ought to have been exhilarating, but it wasn't.

He was confident, all right; but not very happy.

8

The road was wet, and the light from headlamps splashed confusingly at corners, blurring across the windscreen. The wipers ticked to and fro. Roger lit a cigarette with one hand and pressed his foot down harder on the accelerator.

The country ahead was dark, spotted only here and there with a glimmer of light from farms or clusters of distant houses. The rain flickered like a bead curtain, into which the car plunged.

There were few people on the road tonight. Only, every now and then, a rattling farm lorry swung out of a side road, or a local bus lumbered up towards him and went past hissing in wetness, its frieze of light like a ship rocking through the dark.

And, every now and then, in his mirror he caught a glimpse of headlamps a long way behind.

It was not until he was within twenty

miles of Easterdyke that he seriously began to wonder if he were being followed.

There was no reason why another car should not use this road all the way from London to the coast. Plenty of people lived down here or paid visits to the district. So Roger said to himself, and slowed. Let the car overtake him and go its way.

The lights drew closer now; then fell back.

He dropped to a crawl approaching the crossroads where he normally went straight on. The road to the left was a minor one: he had once taken it by mistake, and found himself winding back towards the main road for London, twisting and turning through tiny villages and patches of woodland. Nobody who knew the district would turn left here.

He swung the wheel, and turned left.

The road twisted so sharply between hedges and under trees that he could not see the lights behind him for some little while. Then, as he slowed along a straight stretch, the two bright eyes came into view.

Roger felt a brief twitch of panic. His

cigarette burned down hot to his lips. He flicked it out into the rain, and accelerated.

If there were a side road soon, he might reach it under cover of the hedges and race down it, leaving them to go straight on. But they would have a fifty-fifty chance of guessing right which way he had gone.

Anyway, he might drive into a lane which petered out in some field. So many of them did, round here.

But then what would happen? Nobody could be after him for anything serious. He knew nothing, possessed nothing worth having, was in no secrets.

Except that he knew where his father was.

But . . .

He drove on automatically while vague shapes and threats uncoiled in his mind. He was only guessing. Just because a car happened to be taking the same road — perhaps because the driver was lost, and thought that the car ahead was bound to be going to somewhere reasonably big — he was letting himself imagine things.

A building loomed up out of the rain.

Standing on the grass verge was an inn sign.

Roger slid in to the side of the road. A few seconds later he was in the saloon bar drinking a large Scotch. The place was surprisingly full. Men must trudge here from houses scattered around the district. There was a warming, reassuring buzz of conversation.

He drank, watching the door.

The swish of tyres was audible along the road. It came closer, slowed, and stopped.

There was a long pause. The door of the saloon opened part of the way, stayed open for a moment, then closed again. This was followed by the thump of the door into the public bar.

The two bars were divided by the shelves of bottles between. There was an opening at each end. The landlord walked round, sometimes appearing at one end, sometimes at the other, not unlike a figure from a little weather-house, popping out at alternate ends.

Roger half turned. He saw the shoulder of a man in a raincoat, leaning on the bar.

Beyond it was the profile of another — a lean, ordinary face.

Roger waited for five minutes, his fingers warming and growing damp on the glass. Then he moved out of sight, edging across the room towards the far window.

The men moved. They appeared in the opening at the other end of the bar. Still neither of them looked directly through at him.

He could be making it all up. This business was getting him jittery. Waiting for Paula Hastings to worm the truth out of his father . . . stalling with Stan Morrison . . . living on his nerves, anticipating every day that something would go irreparably wrong . . .

He went back to the counter and ordered another drink — loudly. On the other side of the shelves, a minute later, there was the clink of a glass and a voice said: 'Same again.'

Roger downed his drink in one gulp and went swiftly to the door. He slipped into the driving seat, trembling, and tried to make his hands and feet work fast.

It was not until the engine stuttered into life that he realized his pursuers might have fixed it, or punctured his tyres. But they had not done so. He drew away fast, and raced through the small village that lay immediately ahead.

They had not wanted to immobilize the car. All they wanted was to find out where he was going.

He looked up into his mirror. Were two men coming out of the public bar and climbing into their car? It was already too far away to be sure; and then the end of the village main street cut off his view.

He drove more recklessly than he was used to, scraping hedges and cutting corners. A man and woman plodding along through the rain with heads down did not see him until the lights flowed up to their feet; then they staggered towards the ditch, arms waving apprehensively.

Roger followed the road until he saw the arc of steely lights over a hillside ahead. Here was the main road, slicing right across country. He vacillated for a few seconds, then drove out on to its exposed surface. Here at least there was a fair amount of traffic. He joined in the procession heading towards London.

Ten miles back, he turned off again. These were unfamiliar roads — he had so far used the same route on every trip — but he knew his general direction, and after a couple of errors found himself within an hour back on the Easterdyke road, further down.

There were no pursuing eyes. He had shaken them off — if they had ever been following him at all.

★　★　★

Rain had not come to Easterdyke until late in the afternoon. The morning had been a pellucid grey, with no breath of wind. The waves rose and fell in long surges, but there was a smoothness in their undulation that echoed the tranquillity of the land.

Sam Westwood got up early. When Paula came in to breakfast, he said:

'It's time you came out in the canoe with me.'

She had never in her life been on the

sea. 'I didn't know you — we had a canoe.'

'We haven't. I borrow it from a young chap along the creek. We sometimes go out together, but the novelty soon wore off for him. I think he's messing about with a motorbike at present.' He glanced at her keenly. 'Unless, of course, you're still a bit afraid — '

'No,' she said quickly. She wanted to be with him. Within these few days she had experienced something that was utterly new: she found herself completely at home in this strange relationship with Sam Westwood. Even knowing what she knew, knowing what lay ahead of her when she fulfilled the agreement with Roger Westwood, she was happy.

If Sam's real daughter had only felt like this . . .

Mrs. Westwood watched them getting ready. Her lips were tight. She was in the plan and she had wanted it this way, but already some strand in her mind had twisted and she was filled with mistrust. Paula had made no contact with Mrs. Westwood: the woman was alternately fussy and artificially poised, and neither mood was true. It was impossible to penetrate to the real person — or was it, Paula wondered, just that she had been too keenly concentrating on Sam Westwood to be able to see what his wife was like?

'Going out on the water on a day like this?' she rasped. 'You'll catch your deaths.'

'It's a glorious day,' said Sam. He looked like an irrepressible boy defying his haggard mother — yet there was nothing jovial or exuberant in his manner. He merely did what he wanted to do, and let arguments or protests fall away around him. 'It'll be beautifully calm along the creek.'

He was right. Coarse reeds stood up from the water without a tremor. The grasses along the edge, faded to a winter pallor, were still. As the canoe nosed away from the decrepit landing-stage, the plop of paddles was the only sound until the first faint wave reached the bank and started the reeds whispering.

The canoe was a two-seater, painted

blue. Paula found it alarming to be so close to the water: it seemed that the slightest rocking motion would dip one side or another below the surface. But Sam, behind her, said: 'We've been out to sea in this. Rides like a seagull.' He matched his paddle as closely as possible to her uneven, clumsy rhythm. 'All right?'

'Fine,' she said.

She soon fell into the swing of the movement. Gently she swayed, plunging the double-ended paddle in to the right, to the left, watching the bow ripple and feeling the light body of the canoe quiver around her as she and Sam dipped vigorously together — dipped and thrust, urging the blue shell down the creek towards the sea.

He was humming gently to himself. Every now and then he rested, and she rested with him, hypnotized by the broadening spread of smooth water into which they were gliding. The greyness of the world was soothing. It was a cold day, but not too cold: in slacks and a pullover she felt warm and indifferent, skimming without problems, without a past or future, across this clouded mirror.

Sam said: 'Reminds you of the old days?'

'The old days,' she said doubtfully. She was reluctant to be dragged back to awareness of her position, to the need for concentration and calculation. 'Well . . . '

'The boat,' he reminded her, 'at Bray.'

'Yes, of course.' It was surely safe to add: 'This is a size or two smaller, though.'

Sam's stroke slowed. His paddle rose from the water and lay across the canoe. Water pattered from the blades.

'Do you mind it being so much smaller?'

'No,' said Paula; 'I like it.'

'A lot of things must seem . . . contracted.'

Not being able to see his face, she could not tell whether there was any special meaning in the words. His voice conveyed nothing: it was the usual level whisper, echoing the reeds along the creek.

She said: 'It doesn't do any harm to live like this — for a while.'

She had not meant to add the last three words, but they were suddenly forced out of her. It was as though Roger had stood behind her and twisted her arm, insisting that she acted instead of simply drifting.

As soon as she had spoken, she drove her paddle down. On the second stroke Sam was with her. Ahead of them the green banks splayed out and the creek was swallowed up into the sea.

'You think it's time we had a change?' Sam asked.

'Mother won't be happy until — '

'Your mother,' he said, 'won't be happy whatever happens.' It sounded curt and callous; but he went on unexpectedly: 'That's my fault. A lot of things are my fault.'

'But — '

'Never mind.' He was increasing the tempo. Their paddles clattered together, and the canoe rocked until they were in unison again. 'Forget it. Don't spoil the morning.'

She was glad to be a coward. She was glad to preserve the cool contentment of the morning and to drive the canoe forward, feeling the play of her muscles and the leaping vitality of the light craft.

It was fantastic that she should feel so safe and secure with him in spite of the falsity of the situation. Questions thrust aside, she could be at ease with him again immediately.

Perhaps — the thought came to her out of the blue — this security was what Roger Westwood was really searching for. Perhaps he had never had it. Barbara had always been the one: it was Barbara who had drained her father of his love and vitality, leaving none for the others.

She could easily hate Barbara.

'Hadn't we better turn back?' she was asking suddenly. The sea was reaching in with long fingers, lifting the surface of the water in a gentle swell.

'Let's go on out.'

'Today? But we'll get turned over.'

'Not in this,' said Sam. 'You can't capsize these things.'

'With waves like those out there — '

'All right,' he said cheerfully; 'let's turn back.'

At once she changed her mind. If he wanted to go out, they would go out. She could not bear to shatter the spell.

She said: 'No. Press on, Sammy.'

He did not try to persuade her, but accepted the decision gratefully. She felt the force of his strokes as the canoe drove on, rising and falling now in a new rhythm. Invisible behind her, he might have been a strong, athletic young man. She could not visualize him as the frail person she had known these last few days.

'Enjoying it?' he said.

'You bet.'

She wanted to tell him more — wanted to explain the full richness of her enjoyment, and confide in him everything about her childhood and marriage and life in London, seeking understanding and wisdom from him . . .

The absurdity of it almost made her laugh. For he would not be able to grasp what she was talking about. He would be baffled by Paula Hastings. The girl in the boat, who was so close to telling him these things, was his daughter Barbara.

I wish, she thought; *I wish* . . .

The bow of the canoe rose, tottered, and fell in a sickening swoop over a wave. Water sprayed around her head as they dived into the trough.

Sam laughed.

'Better swing round. Run along level with the shore, against that current.'

The sleeves of her thick pullover were wet. The cold on her wrists was raw. As the canoe rocked, she missed one stroke of the paddle completely, and fell forward. Her mouth was abruptly full of salt water. She coughed wildly.

Sam said: 'Getting a bit rough. I hadn't expected it to be quite so choppy. We'll go back.'

They were plucked up by a wave, suspended above the waters for a fraction of a second, then thrown dizzily forward. The canoe swung and rolled, shipping water.

'No,' Sam was shouting hoarsely. 'We won't get round. Keep her straight. Head for that wave.'

She drove them towards the oncoming wave. They breasted it and went smoothly down the other side. It was so effortless that she laughed and wanted to sit back. She had time to look round, and see that they were level with the shore. It looked so close — a twist of the paddle, and they ought to be there. But the sea was too powerful and ruthless.

A man was walking along the sea wall, his face turned towards the sea. He stopped; went on; stopped again.

Paula said: 'Isn't that your friend from the inn?'

'Where?' There was a pause. 'Oh, young Collier? I think it is.'

There was no time for further comment. They were tossed high and dropped again. Sam was making swift stabbing movements with his paddle, seizing whatever opportunity offered to keep the canoe turned into the waves.

'Can't get back to the creek,' he panted. 'Head for river mouth below Easterdyke. Get round the groyne there.'

It was terrifying, yet at the same time exciting. The waves were not really very high; the shore was not far away; it was only the frailty of the canoe that made everything so huge and overwhelming. But they could die. It would take so little to kill them now.

The woodwork groaned, and the

canvas made a strange singing sound. Water flooded across Paula's lap. She was drenched. It meant nothing. She drove her paddle down, and still they were moving forward.

The long wooden groyne that marked the entrance to the river seemed to be no more than a hundred yards away. If they could turn the canoe round and inside it without capsizing, all would be well. The heavy surge of the sea spent itself there, and smooth water lay inside the slight curve of the harbour. It was just a matter of making the turn.

From the corner of her eye, as they breasted a wave, she caught a glimpse of Adam Collier. He appeared to be waving and shouting. She could not believe that he was in the same world as she and Sam Westwood: he was a distant puppet, dancing up and down.

They were level with the end of the groyne. Spray licked up the slime-green tower with its lamp column. It was strange to be caught in this turbulence of water when there was so little wind.

'All right,' said Sam comfortingly. 'Take

it steady. Catch that next wave and then pull her round, and aim at the old coastguards' hut along there. Right? . . . Hit it!'

Ten strokes, perhaps, and they would be in shelter.

She drove down. They swayed sideways but remained incredibly afloat. Again, again . . . Madly she wanted to laugh.

Then water hammered down on her head. She felt the side of the canoe forcing her hip over, rolling her into the water, down and under, twisting her round. Her hands gripped the paddle, then let go. She pushed herself backwards, scrabbling to get her legs out from the bows.

There was a splash of daylight, and she sobbed for breath. Then she rolled under again.

She did not know what was happening — whether the canoe was being rolled over and over, whether it had cracked open, whether they were simply being buffeted from side to side . . . all that mattered was to free her legs and escape from the trap.

Suddenly she had kicked herself away. She surfaced, and gulped for air. A wave lifted her with a smoothness that was ironically consoling. Then the heaviness of her sodden clothes began to draw her down again.

A few feet away floated the twisted blue hull, wrenched into a queer new shape like some animal with its back broken.

Paula struck out towards it, and grasped a torn shred of canvas. Her fingers closed on a wooden strut. She pulled herself up and over the floating body, thrusting it down with her weight but still keeping close to the surface.

Where was Sam Westwood?

Air rasped in her lungs. She was sobbing convulsively to herself. She looked round, seeing the groyne a short distance away, but not seeing a head above water.

Someone was clambering along the groyne from the shore.

Then she saw Sam. His face floated, a shred of white wrack on the dark surface of the water, and one arm groped vainly upwards.

She struggled out of her woollen pullover and the clinging wet slacks. The wind, light as it was, bit into her flesh. She waited until she saw Sam again, drifting away from the canoe in a direction that would carry him beyond the groyne and out to sea; and then she pushed herself off.

She reached him in half a dozen strokes, and got her right arm round him, pulling him over on his back. He gaped and gasped, and struggled feebly against her.

They had not been her favourite lessons, those one-hour sessions at Sollenbury Public Baths each week: she had dodged many of them, particularly when rehearsals were on for the school play; but she had learnt enough. She was able to draw him with her as she kicked backwards, bobbing spasmodically towards the drifting, half-submerged canoe.

The canoe grazed her left shoulder. She reached up, missed, got a temporary hold and almost wrenched her shoulder out of joint. Then, somehow, she was holding on as they were nudged and prodded by the confused currents towards the wooden beams of the groyne.

There was a shuddering impact as the canoe jarred into a green, barnacle-encrusted timber. Above it, leaning down, Adam Collier was shouting something unintelligible.

Paula shifted her grip. One leg was ground painfully against the jagged beams. She felt her hold on Sam Westwood slackening. Then she was wedged against an upright, and her toes had found a foothold. Water lapped and spluttered around her, rising in a steady green surge and then hissing away, sighing, down through the criss-cross pattern of woodwork.

She pushed herself up. Adam Collier had his arms under Sam's shoulders and was lifting him free. She tried to help by pushing upwards, but there was no strength left in her.

'All right,' Adam was panting. 'Now you.'

Without him she could not have managed that last scramble. Now that she was safe, she was finished: she could not have climbed the five or six feet to the top of the groyne.

When she got there, she swayed against Adam. It was incredible that anyone could be so warm and, despite his labours, so dry. She leaned on him, the tweed of his heavy jacket harsh against her breasts. Her underclothes were transparent, plastered to her skin.

Adam said: 'We've got to get along this thing to the land. Think you can make it?'

They bent over Sam. He was leaning perilously forward, moaning. He coughed, and spat water. Adam put one hand on his shoulder to keep him steady.

'Think you can manage?' he asked insistently.

Sam shook his head. Gradually he appeared to realize where he was. With a painful effort he got to his feet. Adam held on to him.

Paula made herself stand upright. Her teeth were chattering. She took Sam's other arm, and together she and Adam led him forward. They picked their way over the crosspieces towards the shore. The groyne seemed impossibly narrow from here, running away to a point ahead of them. To fall either way would be to plunge into the water.

The lurching journey was interminable. Paula did not know how they kept Sam on his feet: he was hardly conscious, but there were reserves of dogged determination in him that kept him going. When the collapse at last came, it would be complete.

The wooden arm was, after a nightmarish few minutes, linked with the sea wall. They reeled off the wooden pathway on to solid ground. Sam sank to his knees.

Already there was a car waiting: somebody had seen them and sent for help.

'Good girl,' whispered Sam. They were bundling him into the car. He sagged, then made a great effort. His mouth was quivering with the cold, but from a great distance he said: 'But you can't swim. You never could.'

It was absurd. 'At school,' she groaned, falling into the car beside him and drawing a rug around her.

'You hated it. You never would learn.'

'I hated it,' she said, 'but they taught me *something*. It came back when I needed it.'

He coughed agonizingly, then tried to clutch her hand and squeeze it.

'Barbie,' he murmured. And then, with an oddly querulous note: 'Barbara?'

★　★　★

Sitting in a dressing-gown in front of the fire, she looked much more at home here than he did himself. Her cheeks glowed in the leaping redness of the flames. There had been a book open on her lap when he came in. Anyone would have said she belonged here.

Roger stood over her. 'You mean to say he was nearly killed?'

'We might have been drowned,' she calmly agreed.

'But the things he knows about the stuff — the things we want to get out of him — '

'Lost,' she nodded. 'That would have been the end of that.'

The mere thought of it made him feel sick. All his plans had been so nearly ruined. He wanted to lash out at someone; and his throat was thick with fear.

He said: 'Was it . . . an accident?'

Her chill grey eyes widened. 'What did you think it was?'

'There wasn't anyone around — anyone who could have tampered with the canoe or . . . or anything?'

She was staring at him unwaveringly as though he were some idiotic younger brother who had said something particularly foolish. She did not even bother to answer. He wanted to smash something through that arrogant face of hers; wanted to make her realize — just in case she had forgotten — who belonged here and who didn't.

Something snapped. He began to shout. 'What the hell did you think you were up to? You're not here for a holiday, mucking about in boats. And don't just sit there like that. You were given a job to do. All you've done is . . . is — '

His mother came into the room. 'Be quiet,' she said. 'Your father will hear you. You don't have to yell like that.'

'Don't I? I drive down here to see how things are progressing, and I find he's nearly been killed. And here she is, taking it easy, not a care in the world.' He leaned threateningly over Paula. 'Has he said anything yet? Have you got anything out of him?'

He had lowered his voice, but he could still feel the shuddering of rage within himself. And she went on looking up at him as though he had no business to be here.

'Not a word,' she said. 'Not yet.'

His mother said: 'It was a mistake. The whole thing was a mistake. It sounded all right at the time, but it's not going to work.'

'Who says it's not?' he demanded.

'She's up to something.' His mother was staring vindictively at Paula.

Roger did not know what she was talking about. Then he seemed to see Paula for the first time since his return. The dressing-gown fell away from her throat and shoulders. The line of her neck was emphasized by the fact that she had drawn her wet hair up into a bun at the back of her head after washing the salt out of it.

His mother's gaze awoke in him the

awareness of the shape of Paula's body — of its breathing existence here, in this house. He shivered once, instinctively. And then he understood what else she meant.

He said: 'You don't mean you think . . . for heaven's sake, what's got into you?'

'There's something going on,' she said sullenly.

'But he thinks this is Barbara. You must be out of your mind.'

Paula lowered her eyes at last. Incredulity flecked her brow with light furrows. As though to herself she said: 'You're all of you out of your mind, I think.'

Somewhere far away a car snarled on a bend, spitting its sound across the evening. He thought of the car that had pursued him; and then of the fact that his father had very nearly been drowned. The urgency of it all seemed to be clamouring in his ears. He said tensely:

'You've got to work fast. He accepts you by now. I want action. We made a bargain — '

'I shall keep it,' said Paula flatly.

'Then keep it quickly. I want results before it's too late.'

'Too late?'

He was not going to tell anyone about the pursuit this evening — if a pursuit it had been. 'Just get busy, that's all,' he said.

'Your father will have to spend tomorrow in bed. Maybe longer.'

'All right. Give him till the next day, then. When he's up and about . . . But why not get a word in tomorrow? You pretty well saved his life, didn't you? Get him while he's in a grateful mood. I'm going to spend the day here anyway, so if I can help at all . . . '

'I don't think you'll be much help,' said Paula.

'You see,' his mother burst out: 'she's up to something on her own. I don't like it. You should never have started this.'

'It's started,' said Roger, 'and we're going to go through with it. Just as planned. But I want some action. Understand?'

Again Paula did not trouble to reply.

He said: 'If not tomorrow, then the next day. After I've gone back to London. But when I drive down again next

151

weekend, I want it all settled — the whole thing. See?'

'Yes,' said Paula, 'I see. And now' — slowly she raised her head — 'don't you think you ought to go up and see how your father is?'

9

Sam Westwood spent the next day in bed. He was not suffering from any serious after-effects of his near-drowning: he just did not insist on getting up, but lay there.

'Always the same nowadays,' said his wife. She looked at Roger as though measuring him up as a scapegoat; as though he might be the one on whom to vent her irritable perplexity. 'Whatever happens, he just . . . just takes it.'

Paula saw the justice of this. She sat with Sam for a large part of the morning, and saw that he was making no effort. He accepted this escape from death with the same philosophy as he had apparently accepted everything in recent years — prison, release from prison, a different life from the one he had known before the disaster. Even philosophy was not the right description; nor resignation. It was as though he had no standards, no way of telling what was important and what was not. He had been put to bed after his soaking in the bitter sea, and he saw no reason not to stay there, savouring the experience in that strangely abstracted way of his. Things happened, and he let them happen.

Yet he was not dull. Paula liked being with him, even sitting tranquilly in his room with him. The pallid November sunlight fell across the end of the bed and struck out at an angle over the floor.

Suddenly he said: 'Who are you?'

She did not move. Her whole body seemed to freeze.

The rescue had given her away. That must be what it was. He had known, somehow, that Barbara could never have achieved that. But he would surely not be too angry: she had saved his life, and at least he could only tell her to leave. Perhaps he was even prepared to laugh about it — she felt sure that in the end he would laugh, or at any rate smile, and she would even be able to share in his amusement. That was how close she felt to him.

She did not speak. She could not. Let

him finish it off in his own way.

'I mean,' he said, 'what goes on behind that melancholy face of yours? I thought you were a queer little creature when you were a kid . . . now you're even more alien!'

He reached out and took her hand as though to show that he did not mean it.

Absurdly she felt the sting of disappointment; she would almost have been glad to face his challenge and tell him the truth and go away. But he had not destroyed the pretence: the game was not yet ended.

'There's nothing so very odd about me,' she forced herself to say.

'No?'

She got up. 'I suppose I'd better go and do my share of the household duties.'

It sounded contrived and pompous. His expression did not change. As his hand fell away from hers he merely turned his head on the pillow and looked towards the window.

'You'll come back later?'

'Of course. Now have a doze.'

'I don't feel drowsy.'

'It'll do you good.'

'I've been sleeping,' he said, 'for ten years.' Then, as she reached the door and opened it, he said: 'What's it like to be awake, Barbie? Really awake, I mean.'

She faltered. Her hand moved over the smooth surface of the door-knob. The question was unanswerable. Then she saw that he did not expect an answer. She went out of the room, closing the door quietly, and stepped quietly down the stairs as though he were an invalid who might be disturbed by the slightest sound.

Mrs. Westwood was waiting at the foot of the stairs. She said: 'Well?'

Paula turned slowly to pass her. The woman's hostility came out like a hot, sour breath.

'He seems comfortable enough,' Paula said.

'Comfortable? He's not the only one in this house who's comfortable. When are you going to produce some results? Haven't you got it out of him yet?'

'Today's the wrong time.'

Mrs. Westwood's face worked painfully. 'How much longer do you think you're going to be here? How many more meals are you going to eat in this house before — '

'Shut up,' said Roger. He came out of the sitting-room. But, although he had defended Paula against his mother, there was no trust in his face when he sat opposite her at lunch. He might not be counting the cost of her stay here, as Mrs. Westwood was; but he was certainly counting the days and the hours, waiting for the truth to be laid in his lap and trembling with the frustration of it.

Paula found it difficult to eat. She was sure that after lunch he would want her to tackle his father. He would drive her into making the attempt today, before he once more went back to London.

Towards the end of the meal he said: 'Just as a matter of interest' — his voice was plaintively malicious — 'what are you waiting for? Everything's going fine. You've got him where you want him. He's all over you. All right. What's holding you up?'

'You told me to take it easy. You told me — '

'I didn't say you were to do nothing at all.'

'I've been telling you,' cried Mrs. Westwood, 'she's up to something. You've only got to look at that sly face of hers — '

'Shut up,' said Roger again. 'I'm handling this.'

It was Adam Collier who saved her. Soon after lunch had been cleared away he arrived to see how Sam was getting on. They talked for ten minutes. Paula sat downstairs with Roger, who stared meaningly at her. The moment Adam had gone, she would be sent up to Sam. In the back of the house Mrs. Westwood was rattling things and moving things — a ceaseless, clattering activity that was devoid of either purpose or pleasure.

Adam's deep voice and his rich, rather pontifical laugh were audible from time to time. Paula, with a magazine open on her knees, filled in the intermittent silences, imagining the rustle of Sam's whisper.

When she heard the bedroom door open she closed the magazine. Roger leaned forward. They both turned their heads, hearing Adam's footsteps on the stairs. A moment later there was a tap at the door and he came in.

'Seems to be coming on fine,' he said. 'None the worse for his wetting.'

He seemed unreasonably large in that room. The place had been closing in on Paula, but now Adam had thrust his way in and was pushing the walls back, his head reaching up domineeringly towards the ceiling. He looked superbly confident, cheerful . . . and free. She would have guessed that he was an athlete rather than a writer.

'Thanks for dropping in,' said Roger ungraciously.

Adam loomed over Paula. 'Doing anything special right now?'

'Well — '

'A good walk would do you good. What about it?'

In any other circumstances she would have shrugged the invitation away. The man was nothing to her, and she did not particularly want their brief acquaintance-ship to develop. But in any other circumstances she would not have been here, and these things would not be happening.

Roger was coiled in the chair opposite, willing her to refuse. He wanted her to stay here; she had her part to play.

She looked as bland and innocent as possible, getting up with a vague smile.

'Perhaps you're right. I'll walk up the road with you.'

Roger followed them to the door as though he might, at the last second, think of some way of stopping her. She waited for the stroke — for the comment that his father would need her, that she ought to be here in case he called. But Adam overshadowed Roger. Something in the presence of this other man robbed him of the power to act: he followed, and scowled, and his fingers were twitching all the time, but he made no move to restrain Paula.

Walking along the road, turning her face gladly towards the rising wind, she felt that she had got away from a prison to which she would never have to return.

The feeling did not last. She knew she must go back. Sam Westwood was there, waiting for her.

Adam said: 'After yesterday's excitement you must long for the calm of London. Oxford Street traffic apart, it's a lot safer.'

He was smiling quizzically in a way that indicated that he did not mean her to take his remark too earnestly: it was a light, deliberately banal opening to a conversation. But there was more than that in the smile. It remained questioningly in his eyes after it had drawn away from the corners of his mouth. She was all at once sure that he was recalling her as she had been yesterday: beneath the warm winter coat she was wearing he was sketching in the outlines of her body.

'I thought all writers had to live in London if they wanted to make any sort of success at all,' she said.

'The most successful writers never show their faces in London if they can help it.'

'You're successful?' she asked.

'In my own particular line, I don't do too badly.'

She glanced up at him. His blunt

161

profile looked, she thought, unfinished: it had been roughly hacked out and then left.

She said: 'It can't be a very active life, yours.'

'It's more exciting than you think.'

'You don't look like a . . . well, a desk worker. Sitting and writing.'

'No?' He grinned over some private joke. 'You'd be surprised how much field work I have to do.'

She knew every step along this road. Two or three times along it with Sam, and she had come to regard it as part of her life. There were no other roads but this bumpy surface linking up straggling houses, dividing on the edge of the town and leading you in to the shops or up to the hill. Adam Collier was a stranger on her own special territory.

'My father was in good shape, wasn't he?' she said.

'He looks frail,' said Adam, 'but he's tough all right. One of the toughest men I've met, I think.' She sensed that he was studying her, waiting for her to turn and look at him again. She put her head back slightly, touched her hair, and concentrated on the squat church tower lifting itself out of the roofs of Easterdyke. 'It must be quite a thing, having him for a father.'

'Yes,' she said; 'it is.'

'Today's the first time I've met your brother.'

'He spends most of his time in London.'

'Like you used to. Perhaps you'll be going back there soon — running up and down with your brother every now and then?'

'We've never been together a lot,' she said.

'For a chap of his age, London's got a lot to offer — he must have plenty of girl friends.'

She detected the note of mockery, and was puzzled by it. She said: 'I don't know anything about his girl friends. I've never met any of them.'

'Never? Not one?'

'We've never been together a lot,' she said again. 'I don't know all that much about him.'

'Not know about your own brother? No, I suppose one never does know much about one's nearest and dearest.'

She began to be sorry that she had come out with him. His airy, spasmodic way of talking unsettled her. With his erratic comments and questions he was like a fisherman making careless, impatient casts one after the other, hoping to provoke one strong bite. But what sort of bite?

They left the road and crossed a gently sloping field. It brought them to the top end of the town. They could pass Easterdyke then and go on across country.

Paula said: 'Let's go into the town. There are one or two things I want to buy.'

'Oh. I was thinking . . . oh, all right . . . certainly.'

His disappointment restored her balance. It was normal, male and flattering. She felt amused and faintly contemptuous.

His hand fell firmly on her arm. A car swept in close to the kerb. He was still holding her arm as they crossed from the green field to the pavement where the red brick houses of Easterdyke abruptly began.

'I shall have to be going back to London myself, sooner or later,' he was saying. 'If you do get back there . . . '

Normal, male. She had a flash of revelation, realizing what his remarks about Roger had perhaps been leading up to. But there was no reason to imagine . . . and anyway it was nothing to do with him . . .

'I haven't made any plans,' she said. 'My father needs me here in Easterdyke. For a while, anyway.'

They walked down a street that was probably colourful and crowded in summer. There were shops that sold buckets, spades, postcards, newspapers, and tobacco. Wind was funnelled up from the sea, smelling of the sea: an invitation in summer, but a cold deterrent today. The line of shops broke, chopped up by a group of yellow-faced boarding-houses with wrought-iron curlicues around every window, and then began again, continuing down to the sea front.

Adam's voice boomed on. He was gauche and apparently purposeless in his wandering remarks; but behind it all she sensed something else, and wished she knew what it was. He was not as young and clumsy as he tried to make out. Yet that might be his own particular affectation: every man who had wanted her in the past had become something different from himself as he advanced — cautious or blatant, coaxing or assertive. The true Adam Collier was perhaps hidden as deeply as the true Paula Hastings. Perhaps unwillingly.

They walked. He spoke, and she answered. At the same time she was thinking of other things. She was involved in more complicated thoughts that she had ever had in her life before. Contact with the Westwoods had twisted everything. She had moved from her parents' black-and-white life through her own confusions into this complexity. She felt herself asking too many questions: she could not believe that any of these people really existed as she saw them.

Roger. Were Adam's hints justified

166

— were they even hints? Belonging to the Westwoods as she did, and yet not belonging, she saw what none of them could have seen or faced up to: that Roger's hatred of Barbara had bitten deep into him, so that now he hated all women. She remembered now the days at the studio. Stan Morrison had not been like Roger. His father pawed women with his eyes; Stan used his hands. Roger Westwood, with his nervous movements and quick decisions, his brusqueness and little twitches of revulsion, dealt with the girls in the studio only as a commodity. Perhaps it even gave him pleasure to organize their degradation so smoothly. But he did not want to touch them.

She wondered — knowing that she would never know — what emotional satisfaction he was getting out of paying her for her part in this present scheme of his. The result apart, the pot of gold waiting at the end apart, what did her impersonation of Barbara do for him?

'I wish I hadn't met you,' said Adam Collier.

It jolted her out of her trance of

perplexity. She had answered his other remarks automatically, without having to concentrate, but this one had been thrown at her with sudden force.

She said: 'I'm sorry. I don't see — '

'You're too disturbing,' he said. At once he was smiling and making a joke out of it — clumsy yet calculated flattery. 'I find it difficult to get on with my writing since you came down here.'

'You'd prefer me to go back to London?'

'I'm going back myself,' he reminded her, 'soon.'

She could not respond as she supposed he wanted her to. It was all too futile. It had to be kept light, casual . . . meaningless.

'Sorry you've been disturbed,' she laughed; and he laughed too, with exaggerated appreciativeness.

For the first time she was conscious of a pang of regret. She wished they could talk naturally. His nearness and strength could have meant something to her — she would have let it become something — if they had been somewhere else; in another time and another place.

If, she thought wearily, they had been two different people. That was what it amounted to.

★　★　★

There was a certain vindictive relish in Stan Morrison's face as Roger entered the office the following morning.

'Somebody was here asking for you yesterday.'

'Anybody special?'

'Depends what you mean by special.' Stan peeled the wrapping from a packet of cigarettes. 'He was very keen to get in touch with you, I can tell you that. Asked for your home address.'

Roger stiffened. 'You didn't — '

'No,' said Stan, 'I didn't give it to him. But he looked the sort of guy who'd get what he wanted in the end.'

There was no sympathy in the warning. Stan was enjoying the implications of the threat.

Roger managed to say: 'I can't imagine who it was. Did he leave any name? Or anything?'

Stan solemnly shook his head. 'Just said he'd be seeing you.' With apparent irrelevance he added: 'Any results from your old man yet?'

'I'm working on him. May get a telephone call today or tomorrow.'

'Better be soon, hadn't it? I mean, if somebody else is after him — or after you, maybe . . . '

The danger hung in the air all day. Every time there was a buzz from the outer office, or a man's voice sounded across the studio, Roger felt the pinch of fear in his stomach. He remembered the headlights that had pursued him through the dark countryside, and wondered what sort of car it had been. He would not recognize it if it came after him again; or if it was waiting outside for him this evening.

It was waiting. It was a fast grey van with its back doors open. It stood a few feet from the office door, with a man leaning over the bonnet. At the end of the narrow street crowds surged towards Leicester Square; lights glowed behind subduing curtains in the restaurant opposite; a woman moved slowly towards the lamp light on the corner, her mauve coat and brown skirt drab against the brighter clash of a large cinema poster on the wall. Roger came out of the office and turned right, and the man by the van straightened up.

'Mr. Westwood?' he said quietly.

Roger turned, then tried to carry on walking, more quickly, towards the crowds and the lights.

There were two men, one on each side of him. The rest of the street was deserted. The girls had left the studio, and Stan Morrison was still upstairs. The noise of traffic and the shuffle of feet was only twenty yards away — utterly unattainable.

'In you go,' said one of the men.

'I don't know who . . . '

His arm was caught and twisted breathtakingly, and he was thrown forward. His knees crashed into the back of the van. One push, and he was rolled forward into the van like a sack. The doors slammed shut. A man leaned over him and held out a knife that shone dully in reflected light from a window some-where outside — a window that began to move, falling away behind.

'Stay where you are, or I'll make it painful for you.'

Roger clung to the floor, being jolted up and down as the van swung round a corner, jerked to a halt, sprang forward again, and then lurched under some arch or bridge that resounded hollowly.

They stopped. It had taken only a couple of minutes.

'Out,' said the man in the back, 'and no bloody nonsense.'

The doors were opened. Another man stood there. Roger estimated his chances of leaping at this shape against the diffused light; and they were nil.

He scrambled painfully out. His knees were hurting abominably.

'Move — fast.'

He was in an alley between a couple of high walls. When they prodded him past the van, he could just see that it was a *cul-de-sac,* with the van almost blocking the only way out. He was jabbed up towards the end, where he stood with his back to the wall.

A torch flicked blinding light into his face for a moment. Behind it, the side lamps of the van were pale but watchful.

'Where did your father put the Mannerlaw stuff?' asked a mild voice with a trace of Northern Ireland in it.

'I don't know what you're talking about,' said Roger. Even as he spoke it sounded stupid.

'We haven't got a lot of time,' said the voice reproachfully. 'Just tell us what we ask you, now, and we'll all be happy.'

There was a pause.

'Well?' said a harsher voice from the right of the other man.

'I don't know,' said Roger. 'Honestly I don't know.' He forced a laugh. 'You'd better speak to my father about it.'

'All right. Maybe we'll do that. If you'd just be giving us his address, now.'

Roger tried to keep his lips from trembling. He wished he could see. The two men were silhouettes against the lamps of the van. The walls around him on three sides shut him off from the world and from hope.

'Well?' came the demand again.

'You'll have to find it for yourself.'

They moved up to him. He smelt the breath of one of them, stale and smoky. When two of them held his arms and pressed him back against the wall, he realized that there was a third one. This third one now moved up between the other two.

'We're a lot older than you, sonny,' purred the Irish voice. 'You'd do well to be taking our advice. Just talk, and it'll be so much easier.'

Roger tried to smile into the unreceptive darkness. The fluttering in his throat was of apprehension, and yet of anticipation. The men's hands on his arms awoke a crazy response in him.

'All right,' muttered one of them. 'All right, then.'

Roger sagged against the wall, waiting. This was the sort of thing he believed in — the essential violence of the world which his father had made and in which he, too, wanted to live. He was the devotee of a cruel religion, unexpectedly caught up as a sacrifice but still, even as victim, believing . . .

Until the Irishman softly sighed, 'All right,' and the reality descended — the reality of agony.

He screamed.

10

'All right,' said Sam Westwood, 'let's have it: what's on your mind?'

They were in the sitting-room. They would not be disturbed. There was not even the usual clatter from the back of the house: Mrs. Westwood had been told that this morning was to be the crucial time, and Paula could almost feel her sitting out there, taut and ravaged, longing for release from her ten-year-old resentment.

She said: 'Am I supposed to have something on my mind?'

'I can see there's something fidgeting inside you. It's not usual for you, Barbie. Usually you let fly at once, no matter what.' His smile was too real and meant too much: it hurt her. 'Are you getting bored down here — is that it?'

'I'm not bored,' she said; 'but — '

'Don't be afraid to tell me. I've taken a lot in the past. It won't kill me.'

Now that she was faced with it, the task

was even more monstrous than she had thought. It was simply not possible that she should be sitting here in a strange house talking to a man who was a stranger, preparing to ask him what he had done with the proceeds of a robbery.

She framed words. When they came out she could not believe that he would understand them: they were gibberish.

'It's not just about me,' she said. 'It's . . . all of us. Roger, and Mother, myself — and you. You and the rest of us.' She stopped.

'Yes?' he prompted her.

'You were away a long time,' she said. This was the beginning of the speech she had rehearsed over and over again. Last night she had hardly slept at all, but had lain awake trying out phrases, practising lines of dialogue in a play that might, when the moment came, have to be written as it went along. 'I don't think you've quite come back to us yet. There are a lot of things you don't understand — about any of us. All of us.'

His eyes soberly encouraged her. He wanted to draw the truth out of her:

would he know, when it was spoken, that it was not the truth at all?

She went on: 'Life wasn't easy. It wasn't what we'd been used to. But we managed. We managed because we thought there was a time limit. When you came back, you would put everything right.'

'You wanted me back,' he asked dispassionately, 'for the money I would produce?'

'No.' She took it very slowly. Now she must act as she had never acted before. She put out her hands towards him in a gesture of love and protest. 'Sammy, you know that's not true. What do you think it was like for me when you went away — do you think I was concerned with money? It took a long time — years — before I began to realize what it all entailed. Thoughts about money came a lot later . . . and they were never as important as wanting you back.'

It rang true because she believed it. Every word was sincere. She was Barbara, and she loved her father and wanted him back.

Even though the real Barbara had

perhaps never felt anything like this.

'I'm sorry, Barbie,' he said. 'Sorry.' She felt the warmth of tears in her eyes. 'And I wouldn't blame you,' he said, 'if you did want money. You were right to expect it. You'd been brought up to expect certain things, and you had a right to go on getting them.' It was not so much an apology as a statement of fact.

She said: 'It doesn't matter now. It didn't really matter then, as long as we thought there was going to be an end to it, sooner or later. But — '

'But,' he finished for her, 'I'm not doing a thing to turn the diamonds into cash: is that it?'

It was impossible to tell how far she was provoking him. She must not spoil everything by going too fast. She did not want to lose ground and have to start all over again. *Look down your nose,* Roger had said. *Make it quite casual.*

She said: 'I can't imagine why you're making such a thing of it.' She tried to laugh, airily. 'After the lean period we've gone through a little of the old luxury wouldn't come amiss.'

'Lean period?' he said. 'You weren't too badly off.'

'We had to make adjustments,' she said, finding herself arguing for the sake of arguing. 'When we moved from the house into that small one — which you've never even seen — it hurt. We got used to it. But it hurt.'

'There wasn't any money coming in while I was in prison, but there was plenty left over from the old days. You ought to have been comfortable enough.'

'It wasn't the same. How — '

'What did you want for, Barbie,' he asked, 'that you couldn't have?'

What would the true Barbara (the false Barbara, Paula wildly thought) have answered; what would she have missed and resented?

Paula said: 'Never mind about me. Have you thought about Mother?'

'Yes, I've thought about her. A lot. In prison, and here.'

'Nobody would guess it.' Some uncontrollable impulse drove her on. This was not what she had expected to say, and she was frightened by the sudden rush towards the unknown. But she was possessed by a demon of truth. 'What do you imagine life was like for her while you were away? She had always had a prosperous life. No questions, no worries — taking it for granted that you ran a respectable business and would look after your family and keep everything snug and decent. Then look at the way it turned out! I was a child — Roger and I, we were both children — but she wasn't a child. She was set in her ways — ways which you'd taught her . . . or at any rate made possible for her. Then you'd gone, and there was a long wait before you came out again. We waited. Mother stuck it out. And now — '

'And now,' he took her up, 'I won't make you all rich again. That's it, isn't it?'

'Just doing nothing,' she cried; 'just sitting there, not telling her, not confiding in her, after she's kept herself under control for so long — '

'Sitting,' he said, 'on the richest haul of many a decade. Mm.'

'I don't understand you.' She withdrew slightly, beginning to take hold of her part again.

He said: 'You are right, of course. I'm guilty of a lot. Particularly where your mother's concerned.'

'If only you'd *talk* to her . . . '

'I suppose,' he said, 'I'd got out of the habit of loving her even before I went to prison.'

It was quiet and appalling. And it was a digression so violent that Paula felt helpless. She could only stare.

Sam Westwood moved. It was only then, as he pushed himself slightly back into his chair, that she realized how still he had been sitting until now. His arms lay along the arms of the chair, hands limp as the hands of a paralytic.

'I was an actor,' he said, 'and I was proud of my acting ability. Have you learnt yet, Barbie, how much of everyday life is acting?'

Hysterical laughter sobbed in her throat, but somehow it was kept there.

'The trouble is,' Sam continued, 'that the pretence grows stronger than the reality. If there ever was a reality. I must once have been a boy, and then a young man, like any other. I must once have been Sam Westwood. But I was fascinated by my own skill at deception. I calculated effects — in everything I did, I struck attitudes and built up personalities that had nothing to do with the real me. At least, at the beginning they had nothing to do with me. And the most convincing fake I ever built up was the Sam Westwood who sat in that office and organized a score of petty crooks into one of the most efficient rackets London ever saw.'

He was smiling — whether nostalgically or in disillusionment, it was impossible to say.

Paula said: 'I know what you mean, but — '

'How could you know what I mean? Even now I don't know who or what I was. Right inside myself, where it all originated, I don't know the reasons. And I don't know when the contrived, specially fabricated Sam Westwood became stronger than the Sam Westwood who used to be around somewhere. I've tried to get back to the other one — I had plenty of time to think when I was inside, and I dug down pretty far — but the only one I remember clearly was the man who sat in that office and planned crimes just for the hell of it. Just because other people were so stupid. Just because it was a challenge, and the original Sam Westwood must have enjoyed accepting challenges. There I sat, and organized things. In the early days I did jobs myself, because I wanted to know what it was like: I had to find out before I could rest content. And then when I found how easy the routine work was, and how many ignorant, badly organized men there were blundering about in the throes of the routine, I visualized the next step — I became the co-ordinator. I laughed — yes, I can remember laughing, that much I do remember — I laughed at the picture of Sam Westwood as a big tycoon of crime. Even a small tycoon. The gang boss — it was something out of a film. But once I'd thought of it, I had to try to build it up, just to see. And it worked. Everything I ever tried to do worked. I sat there, and planned, and the wheels turned.'

'And men were killed,' she heard herself saying.

'Yes,' he said; 'men were killed. Maybe

that's when it became unreal. I mean, that's when the made-up Sam Westwood took over.'

'I don't understand,' Paula murmured. She had no idea now whether she was still playing her part or whether this was herself. She was enmeshed in Sam Westwood's own tortures. 'For you to order men to be killed — I don't see how . . . it doesn't fit.'

'It wasn't like that. It never happened as obviously as that. I moved a lever, maybe — put it like that — and the lever moved something else, and a long way away . . . something happened.'

'As callously as that.'

'Men drop bombs from aeroplanes,' he said. 'They press a button and kill hundreds or thousands. Does the man pressing the button consider the lives that he is blotting out? I doubt it. There is a certain job waiting to be done, and he knows the procedure through which he must go in order to get it done. He is flying in a machine which is a triumph of modern science, he is in charge of a missile magnificently constructed by master craftsmen for one purpose and one purpose only

. . . and there is a certain aesthetic satisfaction to be derived from ensuring that this work of art fulfils its purpose.'

'War is different.'

'Is it? Killing men and women like yourself, against whom you have no personal antipathy? All I did was to make plans, and then when a difficulty arose I worked out the best way of overcoming the difficulty. Then I passed on the problem to the men who worked for me.' He began to frown, as though listening to someone else arguing and trying to catch the significance of it. 'The job was done, and there I was, sitting in my office.'

'While we' — so, she thought confusedly, now I am certainly Barbara again — 'were at home, living on that sort of money.'

He nodded. 'And I don't want you to think,' he added, 'that I'm saying I got pangs of conscience when I was in prison. No brooding and repenting. It's not that.'

'But what, then?'

'I haven't decided yet.'

'And when you do?' In her own ears it was almost a scream.

'When I do,' he said, 'maybe you'd like me to do some talking about the Mannerlaw diamonds?'

'You make it sound like a joke. You're trying to find excuses, and none of them make sense. Trying to make out that while you were in prison — '

'I had such a lot of time for thinking while I was there,' he quietly shouldered his way through her outburst. 'And most of the time I thought about you, and wondered how you came to be my daughter. Or Sam Westwood's daughter. I didn't know whether the two were identical. I wondered who you were, behind the mask that Sam Westwood had painted on you with his money and the demands he made on you.'

'Demands?'

'I forced you into becoming the sort of Daddy's girl you became. It formed the right element in the picture. I insisted that you should be spoilt, that you should make a fuss of me, and then I was doting and incapable of resisting you. It was the essential set-up for the tough, cool organizer who sat in his office and ruled a tight little empire of scruffy criminals. I prodded you about and shaped you just as I shaped everybody else. But when I'd finished' — his voice sank almost into inaudibility — 'I still loved you. That was the difference. I got caught again in one of my own designs — and this was one time when I was lastingly caught. Nothing else — nobody else — ever stepped out at me and turned the tables quite as you did.'

Desperately she tried again: 'Mother — '

'Your mother,' he sighed, 'ceased to exist a long time ago. I wanted her. I needed her. But not as a person. She belonged in the setting I had devised for myself, but that was all. She loved parties, and I saw to it that she had as many parties as she wanted. In my position, she needed the best, and she got the best. She was right for the part: she was beautiful, and in those days she had the manner . . . yes, and I know it's my fault if she's embittered now. But she wouldn't have had it so good then if I hadn't been the sort of man I was.'

'That's no excuse.'

'I'm not saying it is.'

'But if — if that was the way you wanted it then,' she fumbled, 'why don't you want it the same again? Why are you so . . . why don't you care any more?'

'I'm not the same man.' He seemed to be shrinking back and back into his chair, as though to withdraw from her; yet there was something imploring in his voice. 'It just wouldn't be possible for me to go back to what I was. I could never keep doing the same thing over and over again. Even in the old days it helped: no job my men did was ever pulled off in the same way as one before. And the men themselves didn't know the plan: they just took orders. Like with the Mannerlaw job. The results of that, of course, were unfortunate.'

'I know,' said Paula. 'I know all about that.'

'Nobody knows all the details about it. Nobody but me.'

'Such as where the things are hidden,' she breathed.

He stared at her for a long moment. Then he said:

'You're very determined, aren't you, Barbie? You're determined to be hard. I suppose you were too young then to understand what had happened to you — and to me — and now . . . '

'I wasn't too young,' she said, 'to be hurt.'

He was forced to his feet. He stared down at her, then padded across to the window and stayed there, looking out.

'Yes, you must have been hurt,' he whispered. 'So hurt that you couldn't face me when I came out — could you?'

'No.'

'But you came back. You did come back.'

'Roger found me,' she said, 'and talked me into it.'

'A funny thing for Roger to do. Not in keeping with the rest of him.'

Paula said: 'You've never liked Roger.'

'Another one of my sins. No, we didn't get on specially well when he was a kid. It's a funny thing to say about a boy of his age, but even when he was little I never trusted him. Not,' he hastened to add, 'that I ever trusted anyone in those days.'

'And do you now?' she asked softly.

He was silent. In the distance was the sound of a car engine, pulsing nearer.

At last he said: 'No. But it's not the same. Once I distrusted people, and despised them because they were all so twisted one way or another. I had no friends. Didn't miss them. Plenty of men, and a few women, I saw a lot of and talked to and made a lot of noise with. But I didn't trust them — and I was right. It was the same in prison, to begin with. All the little cliques and false friendships, and the warders that you can bribe or think you can bribe . . . It was all so false and so dirty that I curled up inside myself, and for ten years I hardly talked to anyone. I lost my voice: and it didn't much matter. And now . . . well, I still wouldn't trust anyone, but I see that it doesn't make any difference. Nobody's honest and consistent right through. You just don't have to let it matter. Have the friendship while it's there, and to hell with the flaws in it. Adam Collier may be a policeman — '

'What?'

'It's quite possible,' said Sam. 'They'd still like to know where the Mannerlaw treasures went to. Though I don't imagine they can spare a man full-time just to hang about watching me. Anyway, it doesn't make any difference. I like young Collier. I like a couple of old sailors over at Easterdyke, and I often have a drink with a youngster who could be a journalist looking for a scoop. I don't know. I don't care. I'm not going to let suspicion foul up my pleasures. Not any longer.'

The car was approaching the house now. There was nowhere else along this road for it to go.

Sam said: 'Trust . . . ' He paused. Then: 'You're staying, Barbie?'

'If I stay,' she said stiffly, 'things have got to be squared up. You've got to face it. Things can't go on like this.'

He stood with his shoulders hunched as though bracing himself against a savage blow.

'All right,' he said. 'What do you want? What are your . . . your terms, Barbie?'

She winced, but made herself continue. 'You know. You must know. I want what we all want — what we've all been waiting for.'

The car stopped outside the house. If this was Roger, he was going to ruin all his own plans: the impatience that had brought him home again was about to destroy the moment.

'Please,' said Sam. 'Please don't ask.'

'I've got to.'

'I'll tell you, Barbie. If you insist, I'll tell you. But . . . I do want you not to insist.'

She said: 'What have you done with the Mannerlaw stuff? Where is it?'

He did not reply. He watched three men coming up to the door of the house. Paula got up, wanting to grip his arm and shake him. Now that she had gone this far, she could wait no longer. She burned to shake the truth out of him.

Sam said: 'You'd better go out for a walk, Barbie.'

'You promised — you've just promised to tell me — '

'We have visitors,' he said dully, 'and I'd like you to go out for a walk.'

He was leading her towards the door,

one hand lightly but commandingly on her shoulder. Some reserve of strength remained from the past, to be called on when he needed it. He was the old Sam Westwood, not to be argued with.

'I'll go upstairs,' she said, 'and wait until — '

'Go for a walk,' he said. 'Go and see Adam Collier. Anything.'

Abruptly she sensed a threat waiting outside the house. There was a heavy knock at the front door. She gasped: 'You want me to bring Adam here? You want him to come and help you?'

'No,' said Sam. 'Keep your mouth shut. That's all I ask. I can handle this.' His fingers tightened on her shoulder. 'When you come back, you can ask me your question again . . . if you've got to.'

He opened the front door. Three men stood there in a huddle as though sheltering from the rain. But there was no rain.

One of them said: 'Hello, Sam. We've been looking for you.'

'Seems that you've found me.'

'It does, doesn't it? Going to invite us in?'

Sam stood back. The three men came in. They all wore brown raincoats, and two of them had grey hats; the other was bareheaded, with crinkled black curls.

The two men took their hats off, and all three of them looked searchingly at Paula. What she saw in their eyes made her reach instinctively for her coat and brush past them, out into the open air.

When she was a hundred yards away from the house, she felt a sickness of shame rising within her. Shame because she had asked Sam the thing he had not wanted her to ask; shame for doing what Roger had paid her to do; and shame for leaving now, when he was in danger.

She knew he was in danger. But, even if he had not ordered her to stay away, she could not have gone back into that house now.

And at the same time she could not bear to be out here, alone with herself.

11

Mrs. Westwood put her head round the door. 'I thought I heard someone come in.' She looked at the three cold faces that turned towards her. 'Do you . . . is there anything you want? Tea . . . or anything?'

'No, thank you, my dear,' said Sam. 'We'll be all right.'

'Barbara — '

'Barbara's gone out. Just run along. We're going to have a little — ah — business conference.'

She retreated apprehensively, closing the door.

Willie McKenna said: 'That's exactly what we are going to have, Sam. You always did have a clever way of putting things.'

Sam said: 'Willie, where are your manners? You haven't introduced me to your new friend.'

'Sure, you were always one for the manners, too. This — '

'I can introduce myself,' said the curly

haired man with the dark features and the hard, flat voice. 'I'm Dave Legat. These two work for me now.'

Sam nodded blandly. 'Never could do anything on your own, could you, Willie? Or you, Russell. You always needed a boss.'

'Now listen — '

'I'll do the talking,' said Legat.

Sam reached for the cigarette-box on the brass-topped table. His movement was slow enough, but it prompted a sharp jerk of Willie McKenna's hand towards his pocket. Sam smiled, handing the box round. Willie and Russell took a cigarette each, then glanced warily at Legat, whose lip curled.

'All right,' said Sam; 'go ahead.'

'We thought we'd drop in and see you. It took us quite a time to find your address: you haven't advertised it.'

'I wanted some peace and quiet,' said Sam, 'beside the seaside.'

'I'm all in favour of peace and quiet,' droned Legat. Everything he said had the quality of a bleak, piercing incantation. 'Let's keep it that way, for both our sakes, eh?'

'What do you want?'

Willie said: 'What got into you, Sam? After we had to break and run for it — and after we got picked up — why didn't you keep in touch with us?'

'Inside,' said Russell, his left eye twitching spasmodically as it had always done, 'we got messages through to you. You didn't answer. Not a peep did we get from you.'

'And when the two of us was out,' complained Willie, 'we sent in to you. You could have got a message to us. Why wouldn't you be sending us the word how we could find the Mannerlaw sparklers?'

Legat said contemptuously: 'I've told you why he wouldn't.'

Russell fidgeted. 'Look, Sam' — suspicion and resentment had brought him here, but there was a note of respect as he tried almost to plead with the shrunken man around whom they were clustered — 'Willie and me don't think you meant any double-cross. We're willing to forget what happened, whatever it was, and share out now. That's what we want. Maybe something did go wrong — maybe you knew what you were doing. Not trusting anyone: that was always the way you worked, wasn't it? Well, we're all here now. What about it, Sam?'

Sam nodded towards Legat. 'And what part is this character playing? Where does he come into it?'

'I run things nowadays,' said Legat. 'Lots of things. You play along with me, and you'll be all right. Well, Westwood?'

Sam was pale and limp in his chair. Still Russell and Willie shot cautious respectful glances at him. He said: 'Well?'

'What did you do with the Mannerlaw stuff?'

'It's safe,' said Sam.

'All right, so it's safe. Where? Are you going to tell us?'

'No,' said Sam.

Willie McKenna's lean, furrowed face darkened. 'Now look here, Sam — '

'Shut up,' said Legat penetratingly. 'I told you this was the way it would be. You've been making excuses for this washed-out little shell of a man — the big-time operator, that's what, eh? — and you've been scared to look for him. If it hadn't been for me, maybe we still wouldn't have been here. But now we *are* here . . . '

He stood in front of Sam's chair, his arms dangling loosely.

Russell said: 'Don't be a mug, Sam. Let's settle it nice and quietly — '

'You always were a coward, Russell,' said Sam equably. 'You always wanted to get things tidied up without a fuss, didn't you? You were always the dodger, always — '

'Shut up,' said Legat again.

Willie stiffened. Russell blinked and looked from his old boss to the new one, and back again.

Sam said: 'Things aren't what they were in my day.'

'You're dead right,' said Legat. 'Now what about telling me where you put that stuff? We'll see you get a share — a reasonable share.'

'Nothing doing.'

Legat said: 'Get up. You're coming with us.'

'I'm staying right here.'

Willie's hand went into his pocket and

emerged again. A shining blade lay along the palm of his hand.

'Coming?' said Legat.

'You'd never have the guts to use that on me, Willie,' said Sam.

'There's always this,' said Legat. He had a gun in his hand. 'It's lonely out here — and in any case I don't fancy you're one for shouting for the police, are you?'

'You won't get much out of me when I'm dead,' sighed Sam; but he began to get up wearily.

'I've no intention of killing you. But I can shoot you in some nasty places. You wouldn't enjoy it. Now . . . what's it to be? Do you walk now, or come for a ride with us, or — '

Sam's knee lifted the loose brass top of the table. It rose in an arc, clanged against the gun, and fell on its edge on Legat's left foot. He yelled, and dropped the gun.

Willie raised his knife. But he hesitated. The old fear was still strong enough — suddenly demoralizing enough — to hold him back for a second. In that time Sam, wirier than he looked, had pounced on Legat's gun and was standing away from them, waving them towards the door.

'Never did have any time for amateurs,' he said. 'Run along home. And don't come back.'

Breath hissed faintly between Legat's teeth. He ran one hand jerkily through his bunched curls in a gesture of long-established habit.

'I'm warning you, Westwood — '

'Spare me the clichés,' said Sam. 'It's been nice meeting you, but I don't wish to repeat the experience. Out you go.'

'We'll come back,' said Legat. 'We're going to have the Mannerlaw diamonds and all the rest of it. You're not going to sit on it for ever. If we go now, we'll be back when we're good and ready.'

'I'll lay in some canned goods,' said Sam, 'ready for a siege.' He was smiling; his cheeks were flushed with something more than physical exertion. 'But I really think it would be better for all of us if you didn't come back. Find some other ambition. You won't get anywhere with this one.'

Willie McKenna, scowling at his

useless knife, said: 'You can't hold out against the three of us, Sam. We'll fix you in the end. I swear to God we will.'

'Thank you for the warning,' said Sam. 'I'll take due precautions. Now, for the last time — '

'You wouldn't fire that gun,' said Russell uncertainly.

'No?' Sam took a step forward. 'I could fire in self-defence. It's not even my own gun — it's bound to have your prints on as well as mine, Legat, and that would take some explaining away. Let's not play games any longer. I got tired of the gangster game ages ago. Just clear off.'

On his own, Legat might have done something; might have taken a chance. It was there in his eyes, smouldering. But he was infected with the awe and indecision of the other two. When they backed towards the door, he was with them.

After they had gone, Sam sat in his chair for some time, his mouth still puckered in a faint, reminiscent smile.

★　★　★

'As a resident,' said Adam Collier, 'I am entitled to drink on the premises whenever I feel inclined to do so. Will you join me?'

Numbly Paula shook her head. Then she changed her mind. 'Yes. Yes, please.'

He pulled a chair forward for her. She ducked her head under the huge beam that crossed the old fireplace, and sat beside the fire basket. The smoke made her eyes tingle; it was stinging in her throat, faintly intoxicating.

Adam went up the three steps to the little serving-hatch behind the bar. 'Mr. Ingle. I wonder if you've got a minute.'

He returned with glasses, set them down on the brick ledge within the old chimney-piece, and said:

'What's wrong?'

'Nothing's wrong,' she said, trying to sound surprised. 'I was just out for a walk, and it felt a bit cold — and the idea of sitting by a fire was too wonderful to resist.'

Her hand trembled as she picked up her glass. Her fingers tightened.

Adam stretched out one long leg, kicked a log into the centre of the fire basket so that it sparked and crackled; and he said: 'If you're worried about anything — now or any time — and I'm around, you know . . . I'm very fond of your father — like him enormously . . . if you want help, you've only got to shout.'

His bluff ease of manner had faltered for once. Embarrassment and something else undermined it. He took a large gulp at his drink.

The warmth of the fire, the placid cool calm of the deserted room outside the fireplace, the distant sound of someone scrubbing a floor: all these things added up to a cosy ordinariness that was the denial of violence.

But she heard herself stammering out: 'Are you . . . are you a policeman?'

His mouth fell open. He stared at her across the fire that spluttered between them. Then he laughed, and she was sure that the laughter was genuine — yet too hearty, too clumsy.

'No,' he said. 'No, I'm not a policeman. Cross my heart. But what — '

'How well do you know my father?' she demanded.

Now he looked away from her. 'I've only met him since he's been in this district,' he said. 'But . . . I knew his name.'

'You'd read about him?'

'Yes,' said Adam, 'I'd read about him. He's not what I'd have expected. I'm glad I met him. I like him a lot.'

'So do I,' she murmured, half to herself. 'But of course — '

'There's no 'of course' about it,' she flared.

He put his empty glass down on the ledge, and came round the fire towards her. He had to crouch, keeping his head and broad shoulders beneath the beam.

'Something's wrong,' he said firmly. 'Have you quarrelled with Sam? Are you . . . sorry you came back?'

'What do you know about it?'

'Only what I've guessed. Hints — things I've picked up.'

'There's nothing wrong,' she said shakily.

He bent over her, holding her arms. One side of his face glowed in the firelight; the other was shadowed and severe.

'Barbara,' he said. 'Please. I mean what

206

I said. If you want help . . . '

Her head fell against him. She was glad to give up and rest, just for a moment — as she had been glad to sag against him in the cold wind on that wooden groyne, when at last she and Sam had been drawn up from the water.

Comfort. The smell of pipe smoke, wood smoke and tweed. The rough surface of his hand against her cheek.

She pulled herself away. *If you want help,* said his voice distinctly, as though still resounding in the enclosure of the fireplace. But there was a more distant yet clearer voice. In her head she still heard Sam; heard his command: *Keep your mouth shut. That's all I ask.*

'I must go now,' she said.

He looked absurd but likeable, hunched under the beam. He had to back away in order to stand upright, and by the time he had done that she had slipped past him into the middle of the room. A few steps away from the fire, and the chill of the morning struck up from the flagged floor.

'Barbara — '

'I must be getting back,' she said.

'You can stay a bit longer. It's nearly opening time.' He produced an awkward laugh.

'No. I promised — I only came out for a breath of fresh air.'

She looked round for her coat. He helped her on with it, then his arm went around her and drew her closer. She tried to turn her head away, but his lips moved swiftly and trapped hers. For a moment she stood motionless, as though frozen; then her mouth opened slightly, and one arm crept up as though of its own accord to his shoulder.

'Barbara, I didn't know . . . Barbara, you don't really have to go?'

She fastened her coat. It was a heavy winter coat, muffling and enfolding her — an armour against the cold and against life.

Adam said: 'Perhaps you're free this afternoon? I could call for you. We — '

'No.'

She heard herself sounding almost angry. This afternoon: what would have happened by then? What would Sam Westwood have told her by then, and what would they feel towards one another by then?

'Tomorrow,' urged Adam. He seemed to be reaching out imploringly to her as she stood at the door. 'If I call for you tomorrow morning, or afternoon — '

'Make it the afternoon,' she said. Anything to get away. And she did want to see him again: even if it added complexity to the trouble she already had to face, she wanted to be with him again. 'If you happen to be going past at about three o'clock, or thereabouts.'

'I'll be there,' he said.

As she walked out from that spurious warmth into the cold outer world, shame returned. This time it was worse than before. It had been accumulating all morning without her realizing it, and now it poured over her. It was as though the opening of her mind to the consciousness of shame, when she walked away from Sam Westwood's house, had led to a wider breach: all the amassed wrongs of the last few years came flooding through, foaming one on top of the other.

She hugged her coat about her, hiding

her body away in it — the body that she had exposed indifferently to the lascivious, snapping eye of the cameras, and that now had become real to her.

If only she had in fact been Sam Westwood's daughter; but without Barbara's stiffness and the corrosiveness of her pride. If only she had met Adam Collier somewhere else, and had come to him clean and unsullied.

They were new thoughts, and their unfamiliarity shocked her.

She tried to dismiss these twisted ideas, to shake them off; but their talons had driven deeply into her. Unthinkable that she should be disturbed by Adam Collier, whom she hardly knew; yet this was what she was thinking. Ridiculous that she should be revolted by the idea of her nakedness spread over a thousand bookstalls, captured forever on thousands and thousands of sheets of glossy paper. To have saved this revelation for one man . . .

But how could she have known? And how, if she had not suffered as she had done, would she have got to this place? Without the degradation leading her step by step towards that house, this hillside, there would not have been this tremor in her heart.

She blundered towards the road, heading back to face Sam Westwood. The question was still there, ready to be repeated. This time there would be an answer. There must be. And after that she must be patient. With Roger satisfied and Mrs. Westwood satisfied, she must stick it out for a few more days. Then, as Roger had said, she could throw a fit of temperament and walk out once more, never to return.

She thought of what another desertion might mean to Sam. After giving in to her, after giving up his secret, still to learn that she was leaving: how would he look, what would he say?

Her vision was blurred. She was straining so intensely into the immediate future that she saw nothing of the winter countryside about her. The wind sang a dirge that wove itself into her mood. She was even talking to herself in disconnected snatches that the wind, sighing, carried away with it. Sam Westwood and

Adam Collier. Sam, with whom she must stay for a while after she had tricked him. Adam, who was coming to see her tomorrow — Adam, with whom she must spend as much time as possible if the next week or so were to be even tolerable.

But would Adam help? Would it not be worse with him there — another man to be betrayed?

She whimpered as she reached the road. A wild impulse to run away seized her. She had enough money in her pocket to take her to London, where she could disappear. The filthiness of Roger's plan and the mounting importance of Adam Collier could be brushed aside and forgotten. It would not take long. She would become Paula Hastings again.

Who was Paula Hastings?

She stood irresolute for a moment, knowing that she could not go. Not yet. Not until she knew that Sam Westwood was safe.

She turned towards the scattering of houses along the last stretch of road. It was then that she saw the car. It had been parked off the road, partly sheltered by one of the squat bushes that made dark tufts all over the fields and saltings. Now it bumped up on to the road and swung in towards her.

Paula stepped back. The car slowed, and the back door opened.

'Come on inside,' said the Northern Irish voice.

'I don't — '

'Inside.' The gun was in shadow, but she saw it clearly enough. Desperately she looked round. There was nothing; nobody. The nearest house stared blankly into the wind. The sea was deep-throated and mocking today. The man with the gun leaned forward. 'Inside.'

She stumbled, and fell rather than stepped into the car. They dragged her in, the door slammed, and the car jerked forward.

★　★　★

Roger arrived just before lunch. There were strips of plaster across his torn right cheek, and his mouth was puffed up. He came into the house stooping slightly, as though suffering from some gnawing pain in his stomach. Around the swollen, discoloured patches on his face he looked white and sick.

Mrs. Westwood was the first to see him. She let out a thin cry that brought Sam into the hall.

'So it was you,' he said. 'They got it out of you.'

'They've been here?' breathed Roger.

'They've been. And gone.'

'You didn't tell them — '

'I told them considerably less than you did,' said Sam.

'I tried to stick it out. Honest, Dad, I tried. But there were three of them.'

'There were three of them here, too.'

'They got me by surprise. Last night — it took me time to get patched up and get down here. I wasn't able to move until this morning.'

'All right,' Sam shrugged. 'Sooner or later they'd have found out, anyway. They didn't get anything out of me, so it doesn't matter. It's just that I'd hoped for a few weeks more of quietness; even a few months. But it can't be helped.'

Roger slumped into a chair and groaned. He put his hands across his stomach and held on to himself.

Ten minutes later he asked: 'Where's Barbara?'

'She went out when my visitors came. She'll be back soon. We were talking when they got here.'

Roger's hands relaxed their pressure. 'Talking?' he said softly, casually.

'Yes. We were interrupted.'

Roger got up and slouched out into the dining-room. He found a bottle of brandy, and poured himself a drink.

When lunch was on the table he began to worry. There was still no sign of that girl. Surely she would not have walked out. He wished he knew how far that talk between her and his father had progressed. Had his father cut her short, or had those men scared her away? She couldn't have cleared out; she simply couldn't have done it — not at this stage.

He ventured: 'Barbara — '

'She's probably having a drink with her boy friend,' said Sam.

'Do you mean she's hanging about

with that fellow from the pub? I can't say I'm struck on him. And she ought not to go off and leave you. To go off when those men were here — '

'I coped with them,' said Sam. 'I told her to go. Told her to keep quiet. Told her I could cope. She believes in me.'

It was not until the middle of the meal that a faint uneasiness began to show itself in Sam's manner. Roger became aware of it: it intensified his own; but he did not want to be too earnest, too anxious about a sister he had always treated with indifference and even contempt. The act could not be changed at a moment's notice.

'She might at least have given us a ring,' said Sam at last. He got up from the table. 'I'd better check whether she's coming back to lunch or not.'

When he came back from the telephone the alarm in his eyes was tense and urgent.

12

Adam Collier drove his sports car down the sea road at a speed that wrenched at the wheel under his hands. The crumbling edges and cracked surface of the road threatened to turn the car over.

He ought to have driven down earlier. He ought to have insisted on bringing Barbara home. He had known there was something wrong; but she had refused his offer, and he had not wanted to arouse suspicion by being too insistent, too curious.

Suspicion. In trying to carry out his job cleverly and unobtrusively, he had let this happen. And right now he didn't give a damn for his job: that wasn't what counted.

His brakes cried faintly as he jolted to a stop outside the Westwood house. He ran up the path and knocked at the door; knocked again when it was not immediately answered.

Mrs. Westwood came to the door and stared at him with weary resentment.

He said: 'Sam in?'

'Yes, he is, but . . . '

She let the vague rebuff fade out, and stood aside to let him in. She had grown tired of trying to cope with anything any more.

He heard voices through an open door on his right.

Roger was whining: 'But you don't know. You're only guessing. And you're not going to do anything silly — I won't let you.' The whine rose, high and unsteady.

'Who the hell are you to tell me . . . ?'

They stopped as Adam came in. He saw the dark, ugly mess of Roger's face before Roger twisted away and flounced into a corner of the room.

Adam said: 'What's happened? I had to come down. What's happened to him — and to Barbara? Have you heard anything?'

He might have known that he would not get a direct answer. His entry had brought a new element into the situation.

Instinctively the Westwoods adjusted to it — and resisted him.

'Who should I hear anything from?' said Sam.

'You know what I mean. I saw Barbara this morning, and she was very upset about something. She wouldn't tell me what was wrong, but I could tell that she was in quite a state. Something had frightened her, and you know it. You must know all about it, or you wouldn't have been worrying yourself, telephoning me.'

'I only wanted to know — '

'Whether she was coming back to lunch. Yes. But your voice sounds much more revealing over the phone, Sam, than it does in ordinary circumstances.' None of them were sitting down. They stood as though anxious to move away, to go into action . . . to *do* something. Roger chewed at the skin round his thumbnail. Sam was limp, his arms dangling, his eyes watchful — and yet still, in some perverse way, grateful to Adam for being here. Adam said: 'What's happened? Where's Barbara — where *could* she be? You know. I'm sure you know.'

'What are you so steamed up about?' demanded Roger. 'What's it got to do with you?'

'Something's happened to Barbara,' said Adam stubbornly.

'We don't know that anything's happened to her,' said Roger. 'Just because she's decided to stay out for a while . . . Dad was only ringing to ask you. That's all. We know what she is. She . . . she does things like that. It's not the first time.'

'Don't try to tell me — '

'She's stayed away from home a long time before now, just because she was in a . . . a mood about something.' The idea pleased him. He turned triumphantly to his father. 'You know that's true,' he cried shrilly.

It was as though Roger wanted nothing to be done about his sister. He was not merely trying, nobly but vainly, to reassure his parents: he seemed to be hysterically anxious to dismiss the whole thing, to play it down.

Adam turned to Sam. 'For God's sake, man, tell me the truth. I want to help. Can't you see that?'

'We're not in need of help,' whispered Sam.

'I know who you are,' said Adam. 'I know your whole story. And I know that something has gone wrong, somewhere.'

'So you *are* a policeman,' said Sam mildly.

'No, I'm not.'

He recalled the conversation, so recent and yet so far away; remembered Barbara flinging the same question at him.

The telephone rang.

Roger swung towards it with a faint sob. Sam moved past him, plucking the receiver up in his left hand.

'Westwood.'

Roger lifted both arms imploringly, waving in a ludicrous sign language. Sam turned away from him.

'Yes. Yes. You're to bring her back . . . Legat, I'm warning you. This isn't going to help you . . . ' The voice at the other end overrode his whisper. He stood there impotently. At last, with deadly calm, he said: 'If anything happens, Legat, I'll kill you. If you don't bring her back. Kill you — all three of you.'

There was a laugh that the others in the room all heard. Then a click.

Sam replaced the receiver and stood hunched over it.

Adam said: 'Who was it?'

'Get out of here,' said Roger. 'Go on, get out. This doesn't concern you.'

'It concerns me,' said Adam.

Roger giggled wildly. 'Goodness . . . if he isn't in love with her! That's rich, that is.'

Sam drew his hand away from the telephone. He looked up. 'Who are you?'

Adam told him.

'Insurance,' said Sam with a little nod. 'Yes, of course. Any company that had had to pay out a tidy little sum like that would want to know where the stuff had gone. And you thought you'd stick it out down here until you'd got it out of me?'

'I had a deadline. I couldn't stay for ever. But I thought I was getting very close. I felt something was going to break soon.'

'Something has broken all right,' said Sam grimly.

'What? You've got to tell me.'

'You're crazy,' said Roger. 'You don't think — '

'I'm not here because of my job,' insisted Adam. 'I swear it. It's Barbara — I want to know where she is, I want to get her back . . . What did they tell you on the phone just then?'

'Only that they'll be phoning me again,' said Sam. 'They . . . just didn't want me to worry!'

Roger's breath hissed in through his teeth. 'Dad, don't say any more. Don't be a fool.'

Sam said to Adam: 'Thanks for coming. But you'd better go now. There's nothing you can do. This is my business, and it's going to stay my business.'

'But you can trust me. I swear you can trust me.'

'I believe you. But I'll handle this.'

Adam said: 'You've got to call the police.'

'It's not been a habit of mine in the past.'

'Good God, man, is this any time for that sort of attitude? You can't get her back yourself. You've got to get the right people on the job. The police — '

'Legat told me what would happen to Barbara if I called in the police.'

'You mustn't do it,' breathed Roger. 'You mustn't do it. For Barbara's sake,' he said.

The whole sound of it was wrong. All wrong.

Adam pleaded: 'Let me come in with you, then. You've got to have somebody. I've got contacts — I can use them without making a fuss. Anything you want doing . . . I want Barbara back.'

'So do I,' said Sam. 'I want her back.'

Mrs. Westwood, who had been standing helplessly just inside the door, not moving and not speaking, suddenly lurched forward and fell into a chair. She began to cry, at first whimpering to herself and then rising to a howl.

Neither her husband nor her son made any move towards her. She might not have been there. She did not look towards them for comfort; did not cry her daughter's name; simply howled.

Adam said: 'Sam, you've got to take me along with you on this. The moment you hear from those scum — '

'I'll see,' said Sam. 'I'll see.'

'Who are they? The men who were with you on the job? If you'd let me start work now, maybe we could have them picked up right away. Take them by surprise. Sam, let me try. Don't just sit here waiting.'

'There are risks I won't take. When they contact me again, I'll find out how to get at them.'

'But — '

'I know that world,' said Sam. 'I've lived in it. I know that men who don't want to be found take a lot of finding. I'm not taking risks until I've heard from them — until I've got something to work on.'

There was icy certainty in his voice. Roger, quivering towards a protest of some sort, lifted one hand and then let it fall again.

Adam said: 'And when you hear, you'll let me know.'

'Maybe I will.'

'You've got to.'

'I shall know what to do when the time

comes,' said Sam. 'And then I'll do it. And I'll get Barbara back.'

* * *

The room had a narrow bed and a chest of drawers. There was a washbasin in one corner which ran cold water only, and beside it was a door leading into a tiny room which held a lavatory, a rusty gas cooker and a sink. The curtains had once had a flowered pattern, but this had faded and been overlaid with grime. A pipe in the wall rumbled unceasingly.

There were two chairs. Willie McKenna sprawled in one, his right hand drooping over the arm. The ashtray on the floor beside him was full of cigarette-butts.

Paula lay on the bed, staring at the grey rivers that twisted and looped across the ceiling. At the same time she was aware of every slight move Willie made.

He quenched another cigarette, took out the knife she had seen before, and began to dig the dirt out from behind his nails. The flicker of the blade as it turned and probed in the pallid afternoon light distracted Paula. She stirred, and turned her face in towards the wall. But then the silence was oppressive. She turned back, and Willie grinned at her.

He said: 'Comfortable?'

She felt that she wanted to be sick; but she was not going to give in like that. In any case, if she tried to dash for the washbasin, she was none too sure that her legs would support her.

The horror of this squalid room was like a poisonous ferment in her stomach. Not the features of the room itself — she had lived for some months in just such a drab place — but the atmosphere that Willie McKenna and the other two had established here: this was the horror. She had to get out. She had to get out before she collapsed; or before these men began to work on her. She did not know what to expect — but she knew it would be foul.

Somewhere outside, in the distant world, a lorry rumbled past and the house shook. The throb of London pulsed through the building, but she was not a part of it.

She looked at the empty chair, opposite

Willie, with the gas fire in between. It was a fairly light chair. If she could get at it, lift it up, throw it at him . . .

He was grinning at her, with that limp, moist grin that was the most sickening thing about him.

'Going to try something, baby?' he said invitingly. 'You do. Go right ahead. We'd have quite a little tussle before you gave it, wouldn't we? And I wouldn't be minding at all. Not at all, baby.'

Paula tried to let her limbs go slack. All she could do was lie and wait. But she remained stiff, her nerves strung to a quivering tension; she was ready to scream. This was not what she had started out to do. She had never imagined, never dreamed there could ever be a situation like this. For a burning second her hatred of Roger Westwood was wilder than her fear of this man in the chair, and those other two men who would sooner or later be back.

There were footsteps on the stairs. There had been movement in the house before, but these were sounds that came closer. A loose board creaked. Willie sat erect, watching the door.

A key clicked in the lock. The man the other two had called Legat came in. In the fading light his dark features looked old and sunken.

He looked at Paula, flipped his key once up into the air, caught it, and sank into the empty chair.

'All right, Dave?' said Willie.

'Sure it's all right.'

'What did he say?'

'Muttered a bit. What you'd expect. Said we weren't going to get away with it.' Legat's laugh was short and explosive. 'Or words to that effect. I didn't really listen. I did most of the talking.'

'You think he'll play it our way?'

'I know he will. There isn't anything else he can do. I told him we'd got his girl. I told him' — he chuckled reminiscently — 'I was ringing him as soon as I could, so he wouldn't worry.'

'That's good,' beamed Willie. 'That's good.'

'And I told him,' said Legat, pushing himself and the chair round to face Paula, 'that we'd be talking to him again, setting out our terms. Give him time to worry.

Let him stew for a day until he gets our demands.'

Willie said: 'And then — '

'Then he'll give.'

His eyes were blank darkness in the twilight. Paula licked her lips and tried to force words out; but she did not know what she wanted to say or could say — to utter an appeal, defiance, contempt?

Legat said: 'Unless, of course, we're wasting a lot of time. We could all save ourselves a lot of time if Miss Westwood herself would talk.'

'I told you I know nothing about it,' she managed to blurt out. 'I told you when you brought me here.'

'It just occurred to me that you might have changed your mind. Lying here and thinking it over, you might have thought it would be a good idea to give me the facts and then walk out. We wouldn't dream of keeping you once you'd told us.'

If she had known, she would have told him. At this moment she would have done anything to get away.

Willie suddenly pushed himself out of his chair and sauntered towards the light switch. The bulb hanging from the ceiling, beneath a dusty yellow porcelain shade, flashed into harsh life. Willie crossed the room and drew the curtains, shutting out what was left of the day.

Freedom now seemed even more irrevocably shut out. Paula could not help looking once, longingly, at the door. To be able to open it and walk out . . . to be free, lost in the wonderful impersonal vastness of London . . .

She cried out: 'This won't do you any good. It isn't going to help you.'

'That's what your father said,' smiled Legat.

She said: 'He's not my father.'

Willie McKenna whistled derisively. Legat shielded his eyes against the light and studied Paula curiously.

'Can it be,' he drawled, 'that we are about to unveil secrets of the Westwoods' married life? I don't know what the estimable Sam would think of a remark like that.'

'I mean I'm only posing as his daughter,' she cried. She sat up on the edge of the bed, pressing down with her hands on the blanket. 'It's all a fake. His real daughter ran away, and because we — they — wanted to find out where the diamonds were hidden, I impersonated her.'

'That's a pretty one, to be sure,' said Willie.

'It's true. I can prove it's true.'

'Can you?' said Legat. 'How?'

She sat there pinned in their mocking gaze. How to prove it? It ought not to be impossible. She could give a couple of addresses — tell them to look at pictures of herself in magazines . . . of course, she desperately thought, it only needed a little insistence until, just to stifle their uneasiness, they checked up on what she told them.

'Sure,' said Willie, 'and I'm thinking your dear old dad wouldn't be so very proud of you right this day. Trying to wriggle out like that, with a story like that.' He looked genuinely disgusted. 'Ah, now . . . '

Lew Morrison would confirm who she was. Men like this almost certainly had some contact with Lew Morrison. But would he be willing to help her?

Legat said: 'How are you going to prove it?'

And, after all, there was Roger Westwood himself. He would not let his father give the secret away to others. Not after all he had done. Roger would tell Sam the truth now, surely; would tell him that his Barbara had been a fake, and that there was no need to do anything about the kidnapping. Sam would be relieved. Sam would laugh to think what fools these men had made of themselves.

And then what? What would they do with her, finding themselves tricked? How long would they wait, with no word coming in from Sam, before they released her?

If they did release her.

'Well?' said Legat sardonically.

She thought of Sam Westwood. For a second, in a strange flash of revelation, she saw and heard him as clearly as though he had been here with her. It was absurd that he should have taught her the meaning of pride. Just as, unknowingly, he had taught her the meaning of shame.

'You haven't told us your real name,' Legat prodded her.

Willie smirked appreciatively.

'My father,' said Paula disdainfully, 'won't let you get away with this.'

Legat got up, looking disappointed. He had hoped to get more savage amusement out of this situation. At the door he said: 'I'll have Russell come along to spell you, Willie.'

'I'm not in any hurry,' said Willie archly.

'Cut that out.' Legat turned to Paula. 'I'll be contacting your father tomorrow morning. We'll have a very special little chat. Until I've heard what he's got to say then, you've got nothing to be worried about. You're very valuable to us, and we'll treat you gently. And then tomorrow, when I've spoken to him' — his smile was thin and menacing — 'I hope you'll still have nothing to be worried about.'

She did not reply, but tried to look proud and confident.

'Nothing's going to happen to you,' said Legat, 'provided your father acts sensibly. Then you can go home.'

He went out, and they heard his footsteps retreating.

Willie McKenna said: 'But plenty can happen to you if Sam acts awkward. Plenty can happen before you get home. The longer he messes about . . . '

★   ★   ★

Adam tried to work. His camouflage was no more artificial than the camouflage of a chameleon: he was genuinely writing a book on the economics of the post-war world — and he found it an exciting task. A job like this one, that involved a great deal of waiting about, suited him very well. Sometimes he was overworked, sometimes not: he had evolved a discipline that enabled him to go on writing whenever there was a lull, and not to feel frustrated when he was immersed in the complications of a cunning insurance swindle or the pursuit of a thief.

But today he could not work. He could not write, could not read, could not force himself out for a brisk walk.

Sam might telephone. It was unlikely that he would hear anything further until tomorrow, but one could not be sure. And if Sam did not ring, there would be further problems. What would Sam be doing; what desperate steps might he be taking to reach his daughter?

Adam went to the window and pulled the curtain back. Outside was darkness, broken only by a distant rhythmic flash as the lighthouse five miles away sent out its signal. The lights of Easterdyke were hidden behind trees.

Downstairs there was the drowsy, contented murmur of voices in the public bar. A faint thud every now and then spoke of an intermittent darts game.

He knew he could not stay in his room. He was going to go downstairs and have a drink. Then he would have to talk to the regulars, who now accepted him almost as a permanent institution, and he would not hear what they were saying and would not be sure of his own answers.

There was one thing that ought to be done. Whatever Sam might think, it ought to be done.

Adam stuffed his pipe with tobacco. The bowl was still hot from its last filling, and his tongue was sore. He struck a match, surrounded himself with a cloud of smoke, and then strode out of his room on to the landing. The smell of tobacco mingled with the damp, sweet smell of the old inn. It was comforting: it all belonged to a quiet, uneventful world. Adam had worked, planned and waited in many a less pleasant place than this. During the precarious years in Naval Intelligence he had sometimes dreamed of such places.

But nowhere had he felt as keyed-up and apprehensive as he did now.

Perhaps if he were to ring Sam . . .

But he could guess what Sam would say. The dry metallic whisper in the telephone would be as bleak and uncommunicative as ever.

It was absurd that he should feel this peculiar loyalty towards the man whom he had been appointed to follow and investigate. The last few weeks had done strange things to his sense of values.

And it was not Sam who counted. Not now.

He thought of Barbara's clear, smooth skin, and the way she turned her head. He remembered the haunted grey eyes, full of unanswered questions — questions he would never solve if he did not see her again.

Sam Westwood was wrong. Years of criminal life had warped his judgement. Perhaps he could hardly be expected to have faith in his obvious enemies; but Adam knew them better, and knew what they could do.

His mind was made up. This was a risk, but less of a risk than what Sam might have in mind.

He went to the telephone. It took some time to get the call through to the one man he could trust — the one man who would be prepared to be unorthodox, because that was how they had solved most of their problems in the past.

Adam said: 'Hello, Fred. This is urgent.'

'It had better be. Dragging me away from the bright lights like this. Where are you?'

'In the hotel.'

'But — '

'There's no alternative. I've got to chance it. And anyway, Westwood knows who I am.'

'For the love of Pete — '

'Listen,' said Adam. 'His daughter has been kidnapped. Yes. Obviously by some of his old associates who want their cut of the loot. They'll be contacting him — tomorrow, maybe, or the next day. God only knows what he'll do then. And she could be in danger. No, Fred, I mean it. This is important to me . . . Yes. Get on to Inspector Frawley. Remind him of what we've done for him. Now we want something back. No dragnet stuff. No pounding feet that the whole London underworld can hear. But if he can get to Barbara Westwood quick, before those bastards are expecting any action at all . . . '

The dependable, loyal voice at the other end of the wire began to ask concise questions. Adam gave the answers. And behind every answer was the urgent, pulsating plea: Get Barbara back.

13

'No,' said Mrs. Westwood, 'you can't tell him. You mustn't.'

'But we've got to. We're not going to let him give the stuff away to those hoodlums. Not for the sake of a girl who isn't what he thinks she is.'

It was a dank, cheerless morning. They were up early because they had been unable to sleep. Sam was still upstairs, shaving. His wife and son were in the kitchen, moving automatically to and fro, laying the table for breakfast. The frying-pan sputtered on the gas cooker, and a thin wreath of steam was beginning to curl away from the spout of the kettle.

Mrs. Westwood said: 'You don't know what he'd be like. I can't face it. There's been too much already.'

She had never recovered from the shock of her husband being sent to prison and from learning what sort of organization he had been running. It had become clear to her that she had never known him at all; and when he came out of prison that feeling was intensified. She was frightened of the unknown Sam Westwood, and sure that such a man must be capable of anything. Her head shook like that of an old woman as she took up a fork and turned the rashers of bacon over in the pan.

'You mean you want him to be forced into handing over those diamonds — after all I've done . . . after all the time we've been waiting?'

'To get that girl back?' said Mrs. Westwood uncertainly. 'Of course not. But — '

'Oh, the hell with her,' said Roger.

What happened to Paula Hastings was no concern of his. Unless she talked, and the men believed her, and they got in touch with his father. Maybe there would be no ransom demand: only a letter telling Sam how he had been fooled. Or, even if they did find out, they might keep quiet about it in the hope of still gouging the secret out of Sam.

Which they wouldn't be able to do if Roger told his father the truth.

If only he were sure how far he could let this thing go. To say nothing, and let his father reveal where the stuff was hidden — and then, before he could pass it on to the kidnappers, to get hold of it all and defeat the whole lot of them: that was the sort of scheme a really smart operator would devise. It was the sort of thing Sam himself, in his great days, would surely have worked out.

But Roger knew he would never pull it off. It was the kind of operation he dreamed of; it would take someone very different from himself to succeed in it.

His mother said. 'I don't want any trouble.' He remembered her as she had swept through the fine large rooms of their old house, her hair gleaming and her mouth smiling lightly at nothing. Now strands of hair tangled at her neck. She was too large for this kitchen. 'If they leave us some, once they've divided it up — just enough to live on and make some sort of life — that's all I ask now. I've had enough. And I don't want him to know I've had any part in this business of . . . that girl.'

'How do you know they'll leave anything? They may just take him for a ride.'

His mother took the bacon from the pan, put it on a plate with a pan-lid over it, and stood the plate on top of a pan of steaming water. Then she broke an egg into the frying-pan. The kettle began to boil. Roger took down the tea-caddy.

'If they ask for a share in those diamonds,' he said, 'we've got to do something. We can't let them — '

'Your father will decide,' she said dully. 'You might as well stop talking about it.'

'But — '

'It was a bad idea from the beginning. I knew it would never work out. I told you so, over and over again.'

They heard Sam coming downstairs. There was the plop of the lid going back on the tea-pot, the spitting of the frying-pan, the faint protracted singing of the kettle as Roger put it back on the cooker after turning the gas off — ordinary, reassuring sounds, declaring that this morning was a morning like any other.

Sam came into the room. Mrs. Westwood took the lid off the plate of bacon.

They sat down at the table.

He'd got to tell his father the truth. Anything would be better than the prospect of losing those diamonds.

And if, then, his father refused ever to tell him where they were?

Sam pushed his plate away. 'Sorry.'

'You've got to eat something,' said his wife flatly, without affection or concern.

Roger kept his gaze fixed on his plate. If he told Sam now, before the message arrived that might show the whole thing up, at least he would get the credit for being honest. At any rate that fortune wouldn't be handed over to save a girl who meant nothing to any of them.

Across the table his mother put down the tea-pot on its stand with a loud rattle. Her hand was shaking. He knew that she was silently imploring him to be quiet.

But he could not keep quiet for ever.

There was a faint, ghostly, musical vibration; then the telephone began to ring.

Sam half rose from the table, held himself propped up for a moment as though weakness made it impossible for him to move, then walked stiffly towards the telephone.

Roger and his mother stayed where they were. They did not make a sound.

'Speaking,' said Sam.

There was a long pause. Mrs. Westwood leaned across the table. Her mouth worked. Roger put up one hand as though to ward her off. If she had any warnings, any entreaties, he did not want to listen to them.

Sam said: 'I see. Two o'clock . . . No good taking that tone of voice with me, Legat. I'll do what I think best.'

Again there was silence.

Then: 'All right. I heard you. Yes.'

The bell rang faintly again. Sam came back into the room. He did not look at the other two.

Mrs. Westwood was the first to crack. She stammered: 'Well? What . . . what do they say?'

'More or less what I expected.'

'Yes, but — '

'How do they want the ransom,' demanded Roger harshly, 'and when?'

Sam raised his eyes unseeingly. Finally

he said: 'I'm to go this afternoon to the Red Lion at Grenbridge. They'll pick me up there. Evidently they don't want to venture as far down as this, into an exposed area where they can't keep a good watch on things. I'll be watched in Grenbridge, and if there are any police-men or anyone else around, the whole thing will be called off for today — and there'll be trouble for Barbara. That's the way they put it.'

'And when they've met you?'

'I'm to take them to where I hid the diamonds. If I don't — and if they don't get back with the diamonds — the one who's guarding Barbara will . . . deal with her.'

Now, Roger knew, he ought to tell his father the truth. But perhaps if he waited, if he stalled, his father would do something to make it unnecessary.

Sam said: 'I'm going to get her back. And it's got to be done without handing anything over in exchange.'

Roger felt a tremor of joy. He might have known that something like this would rouse his father to action. The somnolent weeks were ended. There was nothing to worry about. The old Sam Westwood was taking charge, and there would be no question of paying ransom and no need to confess the truth about Paula Hastings; and in due course, when it was all over, they could get back to the question of the diamonds.

He said: 'Dad, you can count on me.'

'I prefer to count on Adam Collier.'

'But he's a — '

'He's the only man I can trust in this business. Or if he isn't, I might as well give up.'

He went out of the room, leaving the door open. His wife and son sat in silence, hearing the tinkle as the receiver was lifted, and the faint purr of dialling.

Roger muttered: 'But he can't — '

'I told you,' said Mrs. Westwood, 'that your father would decide.' She began to clear the table, removing plates of food that had hardly been touched. 'As for me — '

'Hush!'

' . . . demand from them,' Sam was saying, 'that I go to the Red Lion in

Grenbridge. Two o'clock. They're going to meet me there . . . ' His voice had sunk into its usual whisper. Roger stood as close to the open door as he dared, but only fragments drifted back to him. ' . . . don't know you. No, don't even risk coming down here now, just in case . . . If you could start off in time to be there for lunch. Get yourself settled and . . . '

Mrs. Westwood clattered dishes in the sink, once, to provide a convincing background, to prove that they were not listening. Then she laughed mirthlessly to herself and leaned against the drainboard.

'If you don't fancy it,' said Sam with sudden energy, 'don't take it on. But tell me. I've got to know right now.'

There was a pause.

'Yes. Thanks. I knew . . . Now, let's get it straight . . . '

The voice rustled down again into a whisper.

★   ★   ★

Adam looked at his watch. Twenty minutes from now he would leave. That would give him plenty of time. He could hardly spend too long prowling up and down in front of the Red Lion, and he did not want to spend too much time in the bar before lunch: he wanted his head to be quite clear.

Catching a glimpse of himself in the mirror, he saw a savage, anguished face. At once he made the attempt to relax. He had to appear at his ease. It would not help to go stamping into the hotel in Grenbridge with a murderous gleam in his eye.

Consciously he let the tension leave his arms and shoulders. With the skill of long practice he smiled, as though thinking about something vaguely pleasant but of no great moment. Only someone who knew him well would have been uneasy.

Downstairs the telephone rang. He heard the landlord's uneven shuffle along the passage.

'Mr. Collier — call for you.'

Adam hurried downstairs. Sam might have thought up some new angle. There would be some last-minute instructions.

He said: 'Hello, Collier here.'

'Hello, Adam. Fred here. A fine fool you've made me look, I must say . . . '

The information which followed was incredible. For a minute it made no sense. Then it began to sound plausible. Plausible enough for Adam to interrupt: 'Look, Fred, if this is true I'm damned sorry.' There was a terse rejoinder to this. They talked for another minute, and then the conversation came to an end.

Dazed, Adam reached out and depressed the cradle. He waited, raised his hand again, and dialled Sam Westwood's number.

Sam answered.

Adam said: 'Sam, I've got something to tell you. Barbara's safe.'

'How the hell can she be safe? What are you talking about?'

'She's in London. She was never kidnapped at all, by the sound of it.'

Sam's anger, when it came, was pitiful in its gasping intensity. 'I don't know what sort of game you're playing — if you think you can pull off something clever and persuade me . . . when I had that call from Legat, and another one today — '

'Listen, Sam. Listen. You're going to be

mad with me. All right, I can take that. You're going to be mad because I got in touch with someone in London and drew the police into this — '

'You did what?'

'I told you it was the best thing to do, and I've been proved right.' Adam shook the receiver as though he were shaking Sam Westwood by the shoulders. 'You spent too long combating the police to realize just how good they are. I know them — I've worked with them, and I know what they can do.'

'If you've endangered Barbie's life — '

'Less than you might have endangered it,' snapped Adam, 'if you'd had your way and gone ahead, and then the plan hadn't come off. I'm telling you, Sam, that there isn't any danger. Barbara has been found. I swear it.'

'Where? How is she?'

Adam hesitated. But what had convinced him must be said now in order to convince Sam. He said:

'All that she seemed prepared to say was that she had walked out on you and she wanted to stay out. She was indignant

251

with the police for tracking her down, and she says that any talk of kidnapping is a lot of rubbish. She made herself pretty nasty to some of my old friends, I gather.'

'Just as Roger said.'

'What?'

'Roger,' said Sam, 'told me it was just another of her moods. You were there when he said it.'

'Yes, I was there. I didn't know — '

'If you want to know,' came the bitter whisper, 'the truth is that she walked out before . . . before I came out of prison. Said she wouldn't come back. It was Roger who talked her into coming back then. And I thought . . . I thought she had settled in — that it was going to be all right. She was a bit strange at times, but — '

'She was very upset when she dropped in to see me,' Adam unhappily remembered. 'She wouldn't talk about it. Then when she disappeared I thought she must have been afraid — especially when I heard about those men who'd been to see you.'

'Instead of which, she had simply

decided to walk out again. Because I wouldn't hand over the Mannerlaw diamonds to my precious family. And yet — I was going to tell her. She went before I had a chance of finishing what we were talking about.' Alarm quickened beneath his despondency. 'This doesn't add up. Why should Legat and those two think they could get away with an attempt to extort the thing from me? How did they know it would fit in — that it would be just the right time to talk about a kidnapping, so that I'd believe it?'

'I don't know,' said Adam grimly. 'None of it seems very nice to me. Maybe, somehow, they saw her leaving — '

'Maybe,' said Sam, 'they gave her a lift.'

His despair was chilling. Adam felt that even the certainty of a kidnapping would have seemed better to him, in some terrible way, than this.

He said: 'Anyway, she's all right. She's free.'

'And she wants to stay . . . free.'

'I want you to leave this to me, Sam,' said Adam. 'I'm going to drive up to London — right away. Let me talk to her.'

'If she doesn't want to come back,' said Sam, 'she doesn't have to.'

'I don't believe she knows what she's doing. She was upset, Sam: I'm telling you that. I saw her, and I know that something was wrong. If it was something to do with you, better let me approach her first. Let's try to clear it all up. It wouldn't do any good for you to go.'

For a second he thought Sam was going to answer that he had had no intention of going. But then the disturbing split, the fear of the other possibility, widened again. Sam said: 'But the Red Lion — suppose you're wrong, and it isn't Barbara the police have found, and I don't go for that telephone call . . . '

'Who else could it be but Barbara?'

'If they're wrong, and Legat really has got her, and I don't turn up . . . '

Adam wanted to tell him not to be a fool. The police could not be wrong about this. Fred could not have passed on false information. But the mere possibility, the one chance in a thousand, was one chance too many where Barbara was concerned. He almost wavered.

Sam said: 'I'm going to go to the Red Lion anyway. You go to London — I'll be grateful to you, and you're right about me not going to see her — but I've got to meet them at Grenbridge. Just in case.'

The telephone mouthpiece was hot and moist. Adam heard his own breath faintly resounding. He said: 'Don't be crazy. That's what they're after. It's you they want to get their hands on. They'll drive you off somewhere and beat the truth out of you.'

'Not if I refuse to go with them. I'm going to meet them, because I daren't not meet them. But before I move from the Red Lion I shall want proof that they've got Barbie. And if, as you say, they can't provide it — '

'All right,' said Adam. 'All right. Do it that way. Tell them you want proof. Stall them. We know they can't provide it. And it won't look suspicious: it's a reasonable thing for you to ask. Then, by the time you're back home I'll be on my way back, maybe. With Barbara, just to make sure they don't really get their hands on her.'

'Don't bring her,' said the dead voice in

the receiver, 'if she doesn't want to come.'

'Leave it to me,' said Adam with meaningless confidence. 'It's all going to be all right.'

He ought to have been happy as he drove up to London. The relief he had felt when Fred telephoned ought to have flowered into something richer. Barbara was all right, and he was on his way to see her: that was reason for happiness.

But he felt depressed. He did not know what he would have to face. Something, somewhere, was wrong. Whatever he might have said to Sam, he knew in his bones that something was wrong.

It had been like this before — this instinctive disquietude, the prickling of dread. During the war and in those complicated months after the war, he had experienced it often. There had been days and nights of tension, carrying out a plan that seemed fool-proof and yet, one sensed, would go wrong. There had been the tracking-down of men who were just out of reach and who, one knew, would always remain just there. Traps failed; plans did not work out; brilliant improvisations misfired. In the war's aftermath of intrigue, instinct was often as sound a guide as any; and in his work since then, it had rarely failed him. Now it told him that there was no neat, happy ending just ahead.

There was certainly going to be trouble from his superiors. This was a peculiar way of carrying out his instructions. Admitting to his quarry who he was, and then helping the criminal to get his daughter back — this would hardly appeal to the Company.

But it was not this that cast a dark shadow over his mind. Sooner or later, he knew, he would have to face up to the consequences; sooner or later he would have to decide what he was doing about the job with which he had been entrusted. But now, as he wove through the outskirts of London, through interminable streets as sullen as his thoughts, the job itself had faded into the background. Only one thing counted.

He parked in the courtyard of the hideous red office block, and hurried in, bursting unceremoniously into Fred's office.

Fred raised his owlish face and blinked

with ominous mildness. The scar on his cheek was white, as it always was when he was irritated.

He said: 'Having a good holiday, Adam? Getting matey with the local crooks, picking up a girl friend — '

'Where is she?'

'Do you suppose we've had her deposited in the strongroom to await your arrival?'

'Fred — '

'She's at home. She didn't want to stay there, but I exercised my discretion and persuaded our — ah — friends to help. We talked her into it. I shall probably have to retire next week.'

'You won't regret this, Fred,' said Adam.

'Won't I? I regret it already. I don't know if there's anything in it at all — and yet I've been hinting that if she doesn't stay indoors instead of going to work, she may be kidnapped. Our friends are beginning to wonder why we don't lodge an official complaint. Or a warning. Or *something*. They won't co-operate much further, I'm warning you.'

'They won't have to. What's her address?'

It was a tall, clean house in a street off the Old Brompton Road. There were little cards with smeared ink beside the front door, each with its adjoining bell-push. Adam tried to make out the names. He was surprised to find the name of Barbara Westwood there — challengingly real, as though she disdained to change her name and hide away.

Oddly, the card and the ink were faded as though the name had been there for months.

A policeman said: 'Were you looking for somebody, sir?'

Adam straightened up. There had been no sign of this policeman as he came along, and no sound of approaching footsteps. But evidently a watch was being kept. Fred had certainly been pulling some strings.

'I want to see Miss Westwood,' he said.

'Is she expecting you, sir?'

The man was oddly like a deferential but very firm butler, incongruously dressed in police uniform.

Adam said: 'I doubt it. I've come from her father. But she knows me. I think she'll see me.'

'Your name, sir?'

'Adam Collier.'

'Ah, yes. It was mentioned that you might be along sooner or later. You won't mind if I come up with you, sir?'

They were taking care of her. His heart warmed to Fred, to the police, and to this constable in particular. Regulations or no regulations, something had been set in motion, and red tape had been quietly snipped. Perhaps none of it was necessary — the Legat threats had all been bluff, and once the bluff failed that would be the last that was heard of it — but it was heartening to see what had been done.

'You come right along,' he said.

The policeman pressed one of the other buttons. A faded middle-aged woman opened the door, said, 'Oh, it's you,' and stood back to let them in.

They went up to the second floor. The policeman tapped on a door.

'What is it?'

'It's all right, Miss Westwood, you can open up. I've brought somebody to see you.'

There was the quiet snap of the catch

being removed from the lock. Then the door opened.

Adam stepped forward. He said: 'Barbara . . . '

Then he stared. Because it wasn't. The hair, sleekly drawn back, was almost the same. The grey eyes were, for a moment, disconcertingly familiar; but they looked back at him without recognition.

'Yes?' she said coldly. 'I'm Barbara. Barbara Westwood. But who are you? I don't think I know you.'

14

She sat beside this large, aggressive-looking man and let herself be driven to the house she had sworn she would never visit. London receded and they approached her father's house.

Not that she was anxious to set his mind at rest. That was not why she had allowed herself to be persuaded to make this journey. The incredible story that this Adam Collier had told her had moved her in one way only: it moved her to angry curiosity.

Occasionally he glanced at her, appraising her and relating her to something or someone in his own mind. There was nothing even remotely companionable in his gaze.

Barbara said: 'Do you have to drive so fast?'

'Yes,' he said.

At any other time she might have appreciated the sleek sports car, the rush of the wind and the thrust of the seat as they swung around corners. Today there was no pleasure. She simply wanted to reach Easterdyke and find out what had been happening.

She asked: 'And Roger — and Mother — played along with this, all the way?'

'I've already told you that.'

'It's all so . . . so cheap. Just like them. No pride, no character — nothing but the lust for money.'

'Funny,' said Adam Collier. 'Roger chose well. She was like you in so many ways. The pride was there. But' — his voice softened — 'there was such a difference, too.'

She sensed the criticism, and resented it, coming from a man who had only just met her. 'What difference?'

He braked for a crossing, growled at a lorry that vacillated on the corner, and swung past it.

'She was different, that's all,' he said.

'You sound as though you think very highly of her,' snapped Barbara.

'I liked her.'

'Although she was nothing more or less

263

than a confidence trickster?'

'We don't know — '

'Whatever you know or don't know,' she flung at him, 'one thing is certain: she was a trickster. What else could she have been? What else was she doing in the house, with my mother's and brother's connivance?'

He did not reply. His inability to answer those questions, even to himself, sat on his shoulders like some evil crouching spirit. It was some minutes later, as though it were a fresh idea, unconnected with what had gone before, that he said:

'She was beginning to make her . . . your father happy. They were beginning to relax together, to rebuild his life together.'

'How charming!' said Barbara frostily. She was not upset — merely impatient with people who could have been so blind, people who had involved themselves in such a shabby game.

'I knew him before she came back. While she was away — that is, I mean, while *you* were away — he wasn't facing up to the world. I knew there was something wrong, and knew your absence had most to do with it. But he never said why you were away; never gave himself away. And then . . . well, then his daughter came back. Or so it seemed. And he began to reach out, very carefully . . . very warily . . . for the reins of life.'

'You seem to take the affairs of the Westwoods very seriously,' she said. 'Where do you come into all this?'

Again he was silent.

After a pause she said: 'You think I had no business to walk out, don't you? If I hadn't gone away in the first place — '

'I've got no right to make any judgements,' he said tersely.

'I'm glad you realize it. I'm not ashamed of what I did. It was right. It was the only thing any self-respecting person could have done.'

He glanced very quickly at her, then back at the road. 'You're Sam Westwood's daughter all right,' he said. 'It's in your face and your voice, and the stubborn way you push your chin out.'

He might have been trying deliberately to insult her. To be told that she was her father's daughter as coldly and distantly as that . . . But she sensed that he was adding things up, doing inconclusive sums, trying to fit pieces of a pattern together.

She said: 'I stopped being Sam Westwood's daughter a long time ago. And I've no intention of going back to being it.'

A long time ago. Long before she had actually left her mother and brother so that she should not see her father again. The knowledge that she would never forgive him had been there all through those later years when she should have been at school with her old friends — the friends she had once had. Through those years when there had been enough money yet not quite enough, she had grown steadily and conscientiously to hate her father. He was a thief. He had robbed her of all the things he had led her to believe she would have. She had tried so hard, had learned how to get her way with him, had become the sort of daughter he wanted — the sort of daughter a man with his money and position ought to have — and then she had found out what sort of a man he was and what sort of position he had held. She had found it out first through whispers, sidelong glances and the mystery of averted eyes. It had seeped through her mother's hysterical tears and through snatches of half-heard conversations between adults. Gradually it had grown clearer; and as it became clearer, her hatred grew firmer.

When she left school she stayed with her mother. As a matter of principle — she could truthfully say it was that. Her mother could not be left with Roger. Barbara formed herself, consciously and calculatingly, into a new person. She adjusted to the new life — adjusted better than did Mrs. Westwood or Roger — and was dispassionately aware of the fact that she was doing so. Her astringent pride strengthened her. The things she gave up, the rich ambitions she abandoned, were still with her in the form of a nourishing contempt: contempt for her father.

She proposed to make herself everything that her father had not been. She embraced her new life with a puritanism that satisfied some natural hardness inside her.

267

It was Barbara rather than Mrs. Westwood who looked after the household, even when she was still in her teens. A remark from Barbara, pungent and often cruel, was enough to bring about a reorganization, large or small. Her mother found it easier to obey instructions; her brother found it easier to keep well away.

Barbara did not deny her own pleasure in watching Roger dabbling in petty crime — or, rather, dabbling in the puddles around the fringe of the underworld. Somehow it proved something to her. He was weak and effeminate, and all his father's bad points were coming out in him.

As for her father's good points . . .

But there were none. She rejected the idea that he had had any. She hated him.

And when it was time for Sam Westwood to return, Barbara decided it was time for her to leave. He could take the responsibility of the household now. She had done her duty — a self-imposed duty, and therefore all the finer.

This was the right time for making the break. They were planning to move to a new house: it would not be possible to go on living in the same district and to try to explain the appearance of a husband and father who had been missing for ten years. In new surroundings they would all feel easier — that had been the argument. Barbara shared the view. She wanted new surroundings: she wanted them to be utterly new, with nothing and nobody left from her previous life.

'I'm not going to be there,' she had told Roger, 'when he gets out.'

She had explained, and he had laughed. She remembered his laugh. It was unsteady and derisive, and did not hurt her at all.

'It's all going to start all over again,' she said with disgust, 'and I want no more of it.'

She did not know what her father had done with the things he had stolen. She did not want to know. There had been a silence, a lull, of ten years; and the thought of his starting in to re-create that lost world — as he would surely do — was intolerable.

'The same old rackets,' she said. Or, with ten years of prison experience behind him, perhaps they would be worse than before. And there was Roger waiting for him, longing to be part of that shabby, crooked organization.

It was not for her. She would not knowingly live on that sort of money, owing allegiance to that sort of man. She would go away. And she would go before her father reappeared. The thought of his face — so dimly recollected now, hardening to a grimace in her memory — filled her with a sick dread. There was no room for the two of them in the same house.

London accepted her. She became a part of it as she could never have done before, when they had lived richly but as strangers up the Thames, drawing their livelihood from the city but not belonging to it. Now she lived and worked in London. Her room was quiet, her life was well ordered. She joined a cinema club, changed her library books every Saturday morning, and was on the Festival Hall mailing list. Her shorthand and typing got her a job, and the man who had taken her on considered himself fortunate to have found her. She was methodical and unobtrusive. She dressed plainly but well; it helped the firm for her to look so expensive and efficient. Anything she did was well done, and she knew it.

'It's like having a man like myself as my own secretary,' her employer said once. Then he apologized profusely. But he did not need to apologize.

Three men in the building made passes at her, at one time and another. Barbara repulsed them all. She lived alone and spent most of her time alone. A young man called Richard, whom she had met at a meeting of the cinema club during a programme of Central European cartoon films, took her out sometimes. She felt she ought to go out sometimes, and his company was pleasant enough. At the end of each evening they spent together he kissed her; she felt it was right to be kissed at not too frequent intervals, and she enjoyed the shy respect he showed towards her.

She had never intended to visit Easterdyke even once. She would not have been able to imagine any circumstances that would take her there.

But the circumstances had arisen. At

271

first she had thought this Adam Collier was mad; then that her father was up to some cunning scheme. In the end she had realized that the scheme, whatever it was, was certainly not her father's. She must go to see him: in spite of all her resolves, she had to visit him in order to clear this business up.

It was all a matter of principle.

However much she might wish to cut herself off from her past, she had some responsibilities. She could not allow impostors to deceive other human beings. A girl who claimed to be Barbara Westwood must be shown up. And whoever had devised this fantastic masquerade must be exposed.

Nothing else would have brought her. Only the necessity of showing the members of her family to one another as they really were; of stopping her father making more of a fool of himself than he had already done.

'Nearly there,' said Adam Collier.

She looked down at the raw wintry coastline and wondered why her father had come here. It was surely not his kind of country. There were no rackets here.

No doubt he was planning to start one, if he had not already done so.

They stopped at last outside an isolated house streaked on one side with faint streamers of green from the sea wind. Adam Collier got out and jerked the door open for her.

He said: 'Let's go and get it over with.'

She found that she was smiling, that she could not help herself smiling. He looked at her with distaste. That made her smile even more. Her lips were drawn back by impatience and excitement.

Adam knocked at the front door. From the speed with which it was opened, it was obvious that Mrs. Westwood had been on her way towards it.

'Barbara,' she said.

Barbara said: 'Are you sure you've got it right this time?'

Her mother flinched and stood aside.

They passed her. She closed the door behind them. Roger appeared at the head of the stairs and came apprehensively down. He attempted a sly grin. Barbara ignored him.

'In the sitting-room,' he said as

nonchalantly as possible.

Adam Collier said: 'Have you told him?'

Roger licked his lips. 'Yes. A bit of it, anyway. He . . . doesn't grasp it all.'

Barbara felt a moment of kinship with the large, indignant young man beside her as he snorted incredulously.

Then she saw her father.

He was standing in the doorway of the sitting-room, and at first glance she thought her sense of proportion had gone wrong. It was impossible that he should have shrivelled up in this way. It was not just that she was a woman now instead of a girl, looking up at him: he had shrunk, and his face was not the face she had remembered and tried not to remember.

'You're Barbara?' he said flatly.

She took a step forward. He peered searchingly into her face.

She said: 'I'm Barbara. I'm here to find out what this story means — this tale of someone pretending to be me.'

He nodded with a heavy sadness, and looked past her.

'Your brother can continue his explanation,' he said. 'We were waiting for you. I

. . . didn't know what to believe. Now I can see. You're Barbara, all right.'

He jerked his head towards the room from which he had just come. Adam went in, and Barbara followed him. She turned to see Roger hesitating, unwilling to pass his father. It was as though there had been a violent scene just before they arrived, and Roger, like a cringeing little boy, had been whipped.

Abruptly he scuttled in, and his mother came after him. Sam Westwood came in and closed the door. He looked at Adam Collier and said:

'I've only been back half an hour. They gave me your telephone message.'

'I drove back as fast as I could. With . . . with your daughter.'

Barbara summed up the room in a quick, penetrating glance. Some of the furniture was familiar, but it looked out of place here. Everything was sharpened — vivid and as unconvincing as stage props. The features of the people in the room, too, were over-emphasized. They stood waiting for a cue.

She sat down, took off her gloves, and

said: 'I think it's obvious that Roger was after your money. That's all there is to it.'

'I had deduced that,' said her father.

Roger moved into the centre of the room, lifting both hands appealingly. 'Now, look — '

'You'd better tell me the whole story,' said Barbara. 'Let's clear it up, so that I can get back to town. I didn't want to come down here. I wouldn't have come if I didn't feel you needed someone to clear up the mess.'

Her gaze crossed her father's. His wonderment brought the smile back to her face; she felt it twitching at her mouth. If he was hurt, so much the better.

He said: 'You'd better tell her, Roger. I wouldn't mind hearing it again, myself. Maybe it will make more sense this time.'

'Well, now . . .'

Roger tried to sound expansive. He forced a grin, flicked it pleadingly around his audience, and then sat down on the arm of a chair.

'Look, Babs,' he said in a sudden rush, 'it's all very well for you. You went and left us to it. You didn't give a damn about

Dad's feelings — about what it would be like for him when he came home.'

'No,' she said very precisely, 'I did not.'

'Well, somebody had to do something for him.'

'Did that include providing a substitute for me?'

Already, in so few words, she had brought tiny tears into Roger's eyes. It was an old accomplishment: she took quiet pleasure in the fact that she was still proficient in it.

He cried: 'If you're going to use that detestable tone of voice — '

'Go on,' she said calmly. 'Finish the story.'

'You're beastly. You always were. If you think *I* wanted you back, you're very much mistaken. But Dad wanted you — it meant a lot to him — so I looked everywhere for you. Everywhere. All I wanted to do was to make him happy and . . . '

'Finish the story,' said his father.

Roger gulped. He glanced furtively around at the watching eyes. This time he could not summon the vestige of a grin.

In a voice almost as hoarse as his

father's, he went on: 'I found somebody else. Mother and I' — he quickened his pace, hurrying on over her whimper of protest and denial — 'thought that if Dad could only settle down, feel really at home, everything would sort itself out. Then maybe we could tell him the truth. And it wouldn't matter then.'

Adam Collier leaned forward, shaking his head.

'This is the craziest — '

'When you talk of everything sorting itself out,' said Barbara, 'what do you mean?' She knew. She was sure she knew. Coming down in the car, she had worked this out as being the only possible explanation. She flashed the direct question at him: 'Have you had any money from the Mannerlaw diamonds? Has our clever father shared out the loot yet? Has he?'

'You weren't here,' cried Roger. 'It's nothing to do with you. You didn't want a share. You said you didn't want any part in it. Over and over again you said that.'

'Did he share it out?' she demanded inexorably. 'Or was he waiting until he could get me home again? Was that what he told you?'

'No,' said her father. 'I didn't tell him any such thing. But he had ideas of his own. He felt that if you were here — and a substitute you was better, even, than the real thing — I would melt. That's it, isn't it?'

Roger did not reply.

'A brilliant scheme,' said Barbara. 'Worthy of his father.'

Adam Collier's head came round. He stared at her. She turned abruptly to confront him. 'We're a wonderful family, aren't we?' she said.

Roger tried to struggle on. 'Just because something went wrong — '

'Wrong?' she echoed. 'You seem to have made a splendid mess of the whole thing. And who was this girl who was supposed to be an adequate substitute for me? What's happened to her?'

'What the hell does it matter?' said Roger.

Adam Collier got up. He towered over the younger man.

'You little bastard — '

'They've got her,' said Sam. 'Ten to one they were telling the truth, and they've got her.'

'You spoke to them?'

'I went to the Red Lion. They told me they had a car ready, and I said I wasn't coming. It was Legat. He started to threaten. I told him I wanted proof that they'd got Barbara.' He looked at his daughter, bemused. 'Got *her*,' he said. 'And Legat got mad. He said he'd give me proof all right, if I didn't play along with them there and then. I . . . I nearly went.'

'It's a good job you didn't,' said Roger eagerly. Too eagerly. He was flushed, looking away from Adam and towards his father. 'You don't have to worry about her,' he shouted in a great burst of relief, as though here he was at last on safe ground. 'All right, I made a mistake. It looks pretty stupid from here. But it seemed good at the time. I hired the girl — all right — and if she wants to, she can prove she's not Babs.'

'Can she?' said Adam Collier.

'Well, if she can't, what the hell? She was

a tart. I know all about her. She worked for me and then went on to Lew Morrison.' He was throwing words at his father. 'You know Lew Morrison. You know what sort of girl he gets his hands on. She's a slut, and we don't owe her anything. She's unlucky, but that's nothing to do with us. Leave her to it. It's a good job you stopped in time, and didn't get mixed up with those roughnecks. Everything's fine. There's been no harm done. None. Has there, really?'

Adam Collier hit him. Roger's head was jolted round, and he fell backwards into the chair. Adam pulled him up with one hand, and hit him again. This time Roger lurched back across the room and hit the wall. He crumpled up and began to sob.

Sam said: 'Thank you.'

'You're very chivalrous,' said Barbara. 'Both of you. This remarkable young woman seems to have made quite an impression on you.'

The two men seemed unaware of her presence. They were looking questioningly at one another.

Adam Collier said: 'She's not your daughter. And if what he says is true — '

'It makes no difference,' said Sam.

'We're going to get her back.'

'Yes.' Sam's whisper was harsh. 'But we're going to have to wait. I asked them for proof . . . and they said I'd have it. What will they do to her? How will they prove they've got her?'

Barbara said: 'In all the most fashionable sadistic thrillers — '

'What will they do to her?' said Sam.

15

Paula had slept in her clothes. She had dozed off in ten or fifteen-minute snatches, each time waking up with a sour taste in her mouth. The room was stuffy, the window wedged tightly shut. The night had been interminable, and the day went slowly.

Willie McKenna sat watching her vacuously, with a permanent leer that had frozen on his face. Willie and the other man, Russell, had taken it in turns to guard her: spasmodically they tried talking to her, but she refused to answer. Now Russell was away with Legat — away getting in touch with Sam Westwood — and Willie sprawled again in the chair. He looked as frowsty and bored as she felt.

She wondered how long it would be before there was some news from the other two. In spite of her reluctance even to acknowledge Willie's existence, she found herself saying:

'I may be here for days. It's impossible.'

'If you're here for days,' said Willie, yawning, 'you're here for days.'

'You've no idea how far they may have to go to . . . to find the diamonds.'

'Not far,' said Willie. 'We did the job not fifty miles out of London, and he didn't have time to go a long way away to hide them. Anyway, what would he be doing that for?'

They waited. Paula closed her eyes and played a pointless, monotonous game: she tried to visualize Sam meeting Legat and Russell, getting into a car and driving into the country somewhere. They got out. Legat took a spade out of the back of the car. Sam indicated a spot close to a hedge, and Russell began to dig. Ten minutes later they lifted out a huge treasure-chest.

Then Legat turned and shot Sam.

Of course it wouldn't be like that. The diamonds wouldn't be buried in a field, and there had surely never been any treasure-chest. More likely they were in a small case in a house somewhere — right here in London, even.

And Legat wouldn't shoot Sam. Murder was too big a risk to run.

They might beat him up, though; and leave him there.

Willie McKenna yawned again, voluminously.

Paula got off the bed and went to the door beside the greasy washbasin.

'Don't be long,' said Willie.

She went in to the tiny, cramped lavatory.

The window in here could not have been opened in years. The place smelt foul. The catch on the window was rusted, and if she tried to open it she would make a noise. 'Don't spend too long in there,' Legat had warned her. 'Watch her, Willie. If she tries anything like smashing the window or anything, let her have it. Don't try to be smart,' he had grinned, 'or you'll have to sit in there with the door open each time.'

Although the window was closed, she had noticed that another smell came seeping in from outside, over and above the stench of bad drains. It was a spicy, burnt, rather sickening smell. This time it was even more pungent than before.

Resounding up the well in the centre of this block of buildings, whatever it was, there came a sudden indignant voice.

'If something isn't bloody well done soon . . . '

There was the clatter of a dustbin lid.

'It's number twenty-five again,' said another voice. 'Them Indians again.'

'I tell you, if half the mugs what go in there could see what comes out the back door . . . '

Paula went back into the room.

An Indian restaurant, number twenty-five. But number twenty-five where? And what good would it do her if she knew?

She said: 'When can I have something to eat?'

Willie glanced at his watch. 'It's only an hour since you had something.'

'I'm hungry. I want a decent meal.'

'You'll have cold meat and cheese next time,' he said, 'just the same as you had them last time.'

'You could send next door to the Indian restaurant for something.'

Willie stiffened. He pushed his feet

against the floor and sat upright. 'How do you know there's an Indian restaurant next door?'

'I can smell it,' said Paula.

He stared at her suspiciously for a couple of seconds, then snorted.

'Not at this time of day,' he said. 'Wait till the boys get back later on. Maybe we celebrate this evening. But maybe by then you'll be in a hurry to get away, huh?'

Paula sauntered towards the window. Willie was at once on his feet, and his hand gripped her arm. She jerked herself free.

He said: 'Keep away from the window.'

She went back and slumped on the bed. This could go on for hours. She lay on her side and studied the repellent wallpaper. The real Barbara Westwood, she imagined, would probably have been hysterical. But the Hastings home had been nothing wonderful, and her life since she had left it had been nothing wonderful; she felt dully that this was just another inevitable stage in the degradation that living had nearly always been for her.

She thought about Sam, and there was a strange sweetness in the memory. In spite of everything — the falseness of her position and the knowledge that she must soon shatter the illusion — she had experienced intimations of happiness, for such a short time.

The happiness, such as it was, had led only to trouble. Sam was going to have to surrender his stolen treasure.

Adam Collier. She wondered how much he had been told about her disappearance.

There were footsteps on the stairs, coming up fast. Willie was on the alert. He turned towards the door. A key grated in the lock.

Willie said: 'Is that — '

'It's us,' said Legat.

The door opened and the two men came in. One glance at their faces was enough. Something had gone wrong.

Paula felt cold inside. She sat up, crouching defensively on the edge of the bed.

Legat stared at her. His expression was not pleasant.

Willie said: 'Did you get the stuff?'

'No.'

'Wouldn't he — '

'He didn't come,' said Legat, his eyes still on Paula. 'He said' — he was speaking very slowly and deliberately — 'that he had no proof we'd got you.'

Willie giggled incredulously. 'Is that the truth, now?'

'He said,' Legat continued, 'that before he would take us and show us where he'd stashed the stuff, he wanted evidence that you were with us.'

There was an ominous silence. All three men were looking at Paula. Their expressions were avid and calculating at the same time.

In a soft voice, Russell said: 'Well.'

Willie's knife turned over like a gleaming fish in the palm of his hand. 'We could maybe send him an ear,' he said with relish.

Paula made herself sit quite still. 'I doubt,' she said levelly, 'whether he'd recognize my ear. Ears are all much alike, you know.'

'Well, then . . . '

'You're all talk,' said Paula. 'That's all it is — talk. You sound like a lot of kids playing Red Indians.'

Willie's lips came together. He plodded towards her.

Legat said: 'Stop the cheap drama, Willie. You're not frightening anybody.'

Willie stood where he was. His eyes were sulky and malicious. Then he murmured: 'We'll see, we'll see,' and turned away.

'Your father,' said Legat, 'presumably knows your handwriting?'

'Handwriting can always be forged,' said Paula.

'All the same, I think you're going to write him a letter. You're going to tell him that there's no fake about it: we've got you, and we don't hand you back until we get our share of the Mannerlaw stones. You can send him your love as well, if you like.'

He was about to say something else, but his attention was suddenly distracted. He seemed to be looking at something above Paula's head. Gradually a smile sneaked across his face.

It was Russell who said: 'That's it. You got it.'

'The hair,' said Willie.

Legat said: 'All nicely packed ready. If you slice it off above the ribbon, Willie, it'll stay all nice and tidy, just the way it is.'

'No,' whispered Paula from her dry throat.

'First of all we'll have the letter,' said Legat. He stooped. She looked down on his almost obscenely curly head. From under the bed he drew a small case, opened it, and took out a few sheets of writing paper. 'Here. Write what I tell you.'

'I haven't got a pen,' said Paula.

Legat glowered, and fumbled in his pocket. He took out a cheap liquid-lead pencil.

'Now.'

'Suppose I don't want to write anything at all?'

'Don't you want to get out of here?' said Legat. He nodded peremptorily at the paper. 'Start writing, or else I'll change my mind and leave you to Willie.'

Paula balanced the paper awkwardly on her knee.

Legat said: 'Write this.' He stared upwards for inspiration, his tongue caressing his top lip. 'Er . . . 'This is to let you know it's true what they say. They've got me, and they won't let me go until you share out with them. Go to the Red Lion at the same time tomorrow, and wait there for a telephone call.'' He looked at Willie and Russell. All three of them nodded: it would have been comic if it had not been so real. 'And you can finish off,' he said, 'with a little warning. Go on. Write this: 'They're sending something to show you it's true. If you don't do what they say this time, they'll make the next instalment worse.' Now, what does he call you — his usual name for you?'

'Barbie,' she said.

'Sign it, 'Barbie', then.'

She signed it. Her fingers were trembling, and the writing sprawled unevenly.

Legat took the sheet of paper from her and read it, silently mouthing the words. He muttered his satisfaction as he reached the end.

Paula saw Willie's eyes widening in anticipation. He was looking at her hair.

Suddenly she whimpered. She put one hand to her mouth, and slid from the bed. Legat turned. Willie took a menacing step forward.

She sobbed: 'Let me . . . I've got to . . .'

She stumbled past them towards the lavatory, and slammed the door behind her. She made a violent retching noise, and heard Russell's snigger outside. It was echoed by Willie.

She made the sound again, and moaned. As she did so, she was holding on to her tightly drawn-back hair with one hand while she loosened the ribbon with the other. The liquid-lead pencil, which she had carried with her as she rushed in was on the window-ledge. She put the ribbon down beside it, not letting go of her hair. It was difficult to hold the ribbon steady as she wrote clumsily along its inner side. She rested the side of her hand against it.

A fist pounded on the door. 'Come on.

Get a move on. You can't go on being sick all day.'

She retched again. And she wrote: *Next to 25 — Indian restaurant.* Then she put the pencil in her pocket and swiftly but carefully twisted the ribbon round her hair again.

They were waiting for her as she came out — like executioners, she thought wildly. She might have been Mary Queen of Scots, or Anne Boleyn, or someone like that. Had executioners then looked like these three — degenerate, lank-faced, detestable?

'Feel better?' said Legat. 'It's not going to hurt, you know.'

She wanted to curse him — to use some filthy, utterly derogatory word, no matter what the result was — but she could only stand there, feeling dizzy and, all at once, genuinely sick.

'Right, Willie,' said Legat.

She turned her head away, not wanting to catch even a glimpse of his face. She heard his quickened breathing as he approached her. One hand rested for a moment on her shoulder, and she knocked it aside.

'Don't touch me,' she said. 'You don't have to touch me.'

'Now, look — '

Legat said: 'Do as she says. Leave her alone.'

She felt the sudden tug on her hair as Willie took hold of it below the ribbon. There was a prickling all over her scalp. Then it was over, with a strange, brittle crackling sound as though the knife had sheared through an electric flex. She felt a final tug, and then was released.

Willie laughed with glee. 'That's quite a hair style you have there now.'

'Give it to me,' said Legat.

Paula forced herself to turn round. She saw the neat brown bun of hair, gathered into the ribbon and then splaying out jaggedly on the other side. Legat picked it up and studied it musingly.

'There's some brown paper in that case,' he said to Russell. 'Wrapped round those tools. Get it out. And some string — just about enough, I think.'

They found a piece of cardboard as well, and packed the hair in it. When the parcel was complete, Legat put his hand in his pocket.

'Where's my pencil?'

Paula sat on the edge of the bed and stared down at the floor, trying to appear dejected and completely indifferent.

Legat said: 'Hey. What did you do with that pencil I lent you?'

Slowly she lifted her head. 'Pencil.'

'That dry pen thing. You know. To write the letter.'

'Oh, that,' she said absently. She shook her head, then reached into her pocket. 'Oh . . . I hadn't realized.'

She was sure that as he took it from her he must get a message through it: it went tingling down her arm and through the pencil into his hand. He must surely guess. When he sat in the chair with the package on his knee and began to address it in tilting capitals, she thought he could hardly fail to wonder. And once he thought about it, he would open the package just to make sure.

Legat said: 'There we are. Very nice. A really nice little present for our old friend Sam.' He held it out to Willie. 'Go out and post this. And bring some food with you when you come back. And something to drink. Drop in on Tony and get him to wrap something up for you.'

Willie went to the door. There he hesitated. 'This means we'll be waiting until tomorrow. More hanging around. And all the time there's no telling what . . .'

'This is the best way,' said Legat. 'There's nothing I'd like better than to go down there again and liven him up. But that could be walking into a trap. Sam Westwood may have called the cops in; he may not. I don't know the way his mind works. But he won't just be sitting and waiting quietly for us to break into his house. We're not going to him: he's going to come to us — with his hands full.'

Willie nodded and went out. Paula watched him carrying that parcel out. Perhaps she ought to have felt triumphant; but maybe nobody would find the message, and if they did how would they know where the Indian restaurant was or where the street was? She felt suddenly lax and deflated.

Russell said: 'Tomorrow — '

'Tomorrow,' said Legat, staring at Paula, 'there had better be results. I'm getting impatient. Very impatient.'

16

They had all been in the sitting-room for an hour before the postman came. Adam Collier had arrived immediately after breakfast — as though, thought Roger viciously, he fancied himself as a member of the family and intended to impose himself on the others. Anyone could see what he was after; he had admitted it himself: it was his job to get his hands on the Mannerlaw diamonds if he could. And yet Sam Westwood did not throw him out of the house.

Roger lit one cigarette from another, and crushed the butt into the tangle in the ashtray.

His sister was reading a magazine. She had her legs crossed, her skirt neatly and smoothly adjusted. She turned over the glossy pages with the very tip of her right middle finger. Roger was sure she was not reading, not even seeing; it was all part of her usual act.

When the knock came at the front door, it was Roger who went to collect the parcel. He carried it back into the room with a feeling of unaccountable exhilaration. He was aware of Barbara glancing surreptitiously at it.

And of Sam — tense, waiting.

Roger put the parcel down on the brass-topped table. His father reached out and touched it.

Roger cleared his throat. 'Do you want me to open it?' He was consumed by a burning eagerness. He wanted to know what they had done to that girl — what sort of thing they had thought of.

Sam snatched the parcel up and began to unwrap it quickly, as though afraid that if he did not go wildly at it he would never be able to open it.

As he spread the brown paper out flat and removed a bent piece of cardboard, Barbara dropped her magazine and stood up.

Mrs. Westwood sat with her head in her hands. Adam Collier took an unsteady step forward.

'Just the way I do it myself,' said

Barbara curtly. 'She certainly got all the little details right, didn't she?'

Roger looked at the odd little knot of hair looped with ribbon. So that was all.

Sam whispered: 'If I'd gone along with them yesterday, instead of asking for proof . . . '

'It was my fault,' said Adam. 'I took Fred's word for it. We all got our wires crossed. I didn't ask enough questions. But you're not to blame.'

'I ought to have gone,' said Sam. 'And today I've got to go.'

Roger said: 'No. This has gone far enough — '

'I've heard everything I want to hear from you,' said his father. 'Everything. Is that clear?'

Roger felt his lips trembling. It had all gone wrong. It could never go right now. Nothing could be saved from the mess. And it was not his fault. It was the others who were to blame — Barbara, who had walked out; his mother, who had no influence at all over his father and couldn't even try to do anything; and most of all his father, who had been such a failure. A failure. Everyone and everything — failures.

Adam Collier said: 'We've got to work this out. More or less the same idea as we had yesterday. But maybe you're prepared to be a bit . . . well, a bit more trusting this time.'

Sam let the ribbon trail from one hand. He looked up questioningly. 'Trusting?'

'Trying to tail you is all very well. I might lose you. They might catch on to the fact that you were being followed on the road: they'll be looking out for that.'

'We can't do it any other way.'

'Why not tell me where you've hidden the stuff? Let me get there first, and wait for you. That's the safest thing.'

Slowly Sam shook his head. 'I can't do that.'

'Why not? Look, that girl's life is important. More important than diamonds —

'You don't believe that!' Roger could not control himself. 'You're real smart, aren't you? That girl's life is important, so please, where are the diamonds? You'll get there first . . . oh, yes. That's what you've been after all the time.'

His father said: 'I told you to be quiet.'

'And let you throw away a fortune? Either you give it to those crooks, or you let this smart guy get his hands on it. All because of a girl.'

'All because of a girl,' Sam echoed very softly.

Roger had to weep or shout. He shouted. 'D'you mean to tell me this is how you ran your business in the old days? You never told me. I never heard that you were known as Sentimental Sam Westwood — but that must have been your name. Sentimental Sam.'

'I told you — '

'The great tough operator — where did I get that idea from? Look at you. Just because a girl — a hired girl, working for me — just because she has her hair cut off, you get all noble. You . . . you . . . '

He saw, from the corner of his eye, Adam Collier moving towards him. He fell against the table, groping with one hand. It touched the hair. In a wild impulse he grabbed it, screamed, 'Just because of a hunk of hair,' and threw it across the room.

Adam Collier came on.

Then Sam said: 'Stop. Just a minute. What's that?'

They turned. The hair now had lost its shape. The ribbon had come loose, and there was a scattering of dark hairs on the carpet. Just like the snippings on the floor of a barber's shop.

Adam Collier stooped, and picked up the ribbon.

'There's something written inside it.'

Sam was beside him. Adam stretched the ribbon out and they both looked at the dark scrawl inside it.

'*Next to 25*,' said Sam. '*Indian restaurant*.'

Barbara sat down again and put the magazine on her knees. She said: 'Not exactly informative.'

The two men continued to look at the ribbon as though it might, of its own accord, divulge further secrets. But there were only those few words.

Adam said: 'You don't remember — places you used to know — an Indian restaurant?'

'I knew plenty. But I don't remember the numbers. And this may be a new one. There must have been a lot of alterations in ten years.'

Adam swung upon Roger. 'You. You work there. You know the sort of place in which those sort of men hang out. Do you know any Indian restaurants?'

'A lot,' said Roger sullenly.

'Do you know one at number twenty-five anywhere?'

'Why should I know the numbers?' He was not even prepared to make the effort. 'I don't eat the stuff myself. I just know plenty of them — all over the place nowadays. Indian and Chinese restaurants, opening up all the time.'

Sam looked again at the ribbon, then at the hair strewn across the floor. He went down on his knees and began to pick up the strands. Roger felt a quiver of futile rage. Here was he, his father's son, spurned and talked to like a child; his sister loved neither himself nor their father; and there was his father down on the floor, collecting bits of hair — the hair of a girl who was nothing to him.

Adam said: 'The message isn't much help, then. I suppose it was the best she could do.'

The best you could expect of a creature like that, thought Roger. It was funny to think that she might easily be within a couple of hundred yards of his London office. All the boys congregated round there — small crooks and big ones, pimps and mobsters and organizers. In his mind he strolled nostalgically along the familiar streets. Before him appeared an Indian restaurant, on a corner. He must have looked at it a hundred times without really seeing it.

It was the wrong one, of course. There were no adjoining houses in which Paula Hastings might be imprisoned.

He realized, reluctantly, that there was only one slim chance of saving the Mannerlaw diamonds. If he could remember a restaurant at that number she had given, if they could somehow get there before his father had to meet Legat . . .

There wasn't a hope of his remembering. Not a chance.

Adam Collier was saying: 'Won't you

call the police in now? They can keep a watch without making themselves obvious. They can be ready to go into action at once. They'll have a cordon round the place, cars out — '

'No,' said Sam.

'But without them, the odds are against us. It won't do. If you're willing to jeopardize this girl's life — '

'The only life I propose to jeopardize,' said Sam, 'is my own.'

Yes, they might easily kill him. Roger half closed his eyes, seeing the room through a blur. It was less clear than the streets of London along which he still walked. Up Dean Street, round a corner. A nod here, a grin there. Once they had wrested the secret from him, they might murder him. They might murder the girl, too, to stop her talking. Not that that mattered.

Frith Street, and a turn to the left.

'This refusal to work with the police — '

'I never have done,' said Sam. 'I'm not starting now. They'd want to know too much. In the end, they'd want some return for their work. And they can't have it.'

Roger said: 'Hardiman Street.'

'What?'

'Twenty-five Hardiman Street,' said Roger, opening his eyes. 'I'm sure of it.'

Adam's hand fell on his shoulder and gripped it painfully. 'Do you know what you're saying?'

'Yes. I can see it plainly. It's one of the few shops in that street with a number over the door. On the glass, in gilt lettering.'

His father's expression changed. He said: 'If you're right about this — '

'I'm sure.' Roger wanted to put everything right. If only he could do it now, remembering the one thing they simply must know, things would be different. He babbled on: 'And the street itself is dead right. There are a couple of houses there that the Spackman mob use. Legat might be in with them — or know them well enough to have taken over a couple of rooms.'

'Which houses?' his father rapped out. 'Do you know? Next to the restaurant?'

'The two on the left, I think. I'm almost positive.'

'If you're wrong,' said Adam sombrely,

'and we went there and bust our way in, and didn't find her — '

'There might be another parcel in the post tomorrow,' Sam finished for him.

Barbara had still not opened her magazine. She sat very primly upright. 'This all sounds so marvellous,' she said. 'Perhaps you can understand why I wanted to get away from this family — this atmosphere. I knew it would be like this. I said it was bound to be like this.'

'You're at liberty to leave,' said her father, 'whenever you want. Nobody's keeping you here.'

'You're not afraid of my being kidnapped?'

'No.'

'I see. You're not the least little bit interested in me, are you? I don't matter any more.'

Sam brushed his hand wearily across his face. 'I don't know whether you matter or not. I can't think it out now. There's too much . . . ' He seemed to brush cobwebs from his brow. 'I'm going to meet Legat,' he said. 'I'm going to take that phone call, meet them where they say, and keep them busy for as long as possible.'

Adam said: 'This address — '

'You'll go there,' said Sam. 'Go there and find it. If you can. Then I leave it to you. Get in, free the girl — and wait for me. They're bound to bring me there.'

There was a silence. Mrs. Westwood stared entreatingly at her husband. Roger groped his way through a tangle of thoughts, all of them dark and jagged. He said:

'Suppose they don't?'

'You mean if they kill me instead?' asked Sam mildly. 'They'll still return to the house to deal with the girl. Unless, of course, they're proposing to double-cross whoever they leave on guard. But that won't make any difference. By that time the girl should be all right.'

'Won't make any difference?' Roger echoed. He had done his share; now he felt justified in letting his anger boil up again. 'You give away the diamonds and say it doesn't make any difference.'

'Whatever happens, they won't get the diamonds. That much I can promise you.'

'But if you meet them and they — '

'I know what I'm doing,' said Sam.

'Murder's too big a thing for them. Especially when it would mean that I couldn't talk. I'm planning on them taking me back to that house. And when we all get there' — he leaned commandingly towards Adam — 'you've got to be ready.'

'I'll be ready. But if I fail — if they get away — '

'They mustn't,' said Sam. It was a flat, savage order that had to be obeyed. 'It's up to you.'

Adam looked at him for a moment. Then, forcing the words out stiffly, as though against his will, he said: 'And then you'll hand the Mannerlaw diamonds over to me?'

Roger gasped.

Sam smiled faintly. 'Let's see about that when we come to it, shall we?'

17

Adam's car nosed into the tangle of streets, jolting to a stop before a 'No Entry' sign and weaving away past a shanty-town on wheels, a street market. There was a welter of 'no parking' signs. Adam edged cautiously in between a moped and a delivery van, and got out. This would have to do.

He strolled along the pavement to the corner, turned left, and went down a hundred yards. Here was Hardiman Street. He stopped to peer in a window cluttered with cheeses, sausages and cans with faded labels. Reflected to his left was the lower half of Hardiman Street.

There were several shops down there. He could safely saunter down.

Facing the Indian restaurant at Number 25 was a small snack bar with a yellowing lace curtain. Adam went in idly, and sat down at a table near the window. A girl in a greasy overall came and mopped stains off the table, and said: 'Yes?'

'Cup of tea, please.'

'Sugar?'

'Please.'

He lit a cigarette and took the morning paper out of his overcoat pocket. Leaning over it, he could look up and out at the buildings opposite.

The rows of windows were drab and featureless. Through the lace curtain he could see the sign over the door of the Indian restaurant, and two adjoining doors. If Roger's guess had been correct, the one on the left might lead to Barbara.

No, not Barbara. Her name was Paula. He could not get used to the idea.

A cup and saucer were set down before him. There were brown lines down the side of the cup, and tea plopped in the centre of the saucer as he lifted the cup to drink.

A lorry swayed past, seeming to lean perilously inwards. Two Italians started an argument on the pavement outside. A policeman put his head in the door, looked round, winked at the girl behind the counter, and went on his way.

Adam made the cup of tea last as long

as possible. Then he ordered another. He was watching the door, hoping that somebody would go in or out — somebody who would help him to decide that this was definitely the house.

But the tall, sombre house remained still and apart from the bustle of the street.

When at last something happened, it took him almost by surprise. The car that nudged in to the kerb caught his attention only when the driver got out.

The driver was a man without a hat; a man with crinkled black hair. He went into the house, and emerged five minutes later.

The car slid away up the street.

Adam got up. More than ever he wished that he had been able to talk Sam Westwood into co-operating with the police. That car could have been stopped before it got to Grenbridge. He had hardly dared to hope that he would get to London before Legat set out; but he had done, and the whole thing could have been wrapped up if only Sam had not been so adamant. The car could have been seized, the girl released . . .

But it was no good worrying about that now. Maybe the police would not have been able to act against Legat: there was no evidence, no ground for an arrest. Valuable time might have been lost in trying to persuade them.

The car was on its way somewhere near to Grenbridge. Sam would have to take his chance, and work out whatever plan he had in that strange mind of his.

At least the house had been clearly identified.

Adam paid for his two teas. He left the newspaper on the table and went slowly out. This was it. He felt the familiar prickling at the back of his neck. His right hand, plunging into his overcoat pocket, touched the coolness of his gun.

He crossed the street and went in at the open door. A narrow stair led upwards. There was a smell of damp and the intrusive odour of curry from next door.

A small man with prominent front teeth emerged suddenly from a door in the shadows below the stairs. He looked suspiciously at Adam.

Adam took his hand out of his pocket. He said: 'Willie?'

The man gave him a long stare. 'There's lots of Willies in the world.'

'Only one who's waiting for word from Dave.'

There was another pause, then the little man jerked his head towards the stairs. 'They've got the room on the second floor.'

Adam nodded, and began to go upstairs. The man watched him until he turned for the next flight. Adam moved quietly. He reached the second floor, and looked along the landing.

There were several doors. In the darkness, relieved only by one grimy window several feet above him, they were all alike. He could not risk making a mistake. There could be no second chance. He had to get at Willie McKenna — or Russell, if he were the one on guard — right away.

Adam retreated, backing away down half a flight of stairs. Then he ran up again, making as much noise as possible. His toes stubbed against the treads. He swayed on the top step, and shouted: 'Willie . . . Willie.' Then he fell forward, letting his body thump to the floor.

Silently he pushed himself up on his hands, poised, waiting.

There was a silence that seemed interminable. Somebody moved downstairs. Any moment he expected to hear footsteps coming up behind him.

Then a door opened in the wall to his left. It opened only a crack; and he launched himself at it.

The door thudded back. Willie McKenna swore, and a knife flashed. Adam's weight carried the two of them across the room, to crash into the far wall. Willie, twisted sideways, tried to lift his right arm.

Adam hit him in the stomach. Willie sagged, but pulled himself free and reeled along the wall. He had still not let go of the knife.

Out of the corner of his eye Adam was aware of the third person in the room. He saw her standing up, heard her say something. There was no time yet to turn and look at her. Willie was crouching, coming away from the wall. Adam's hand went into his pocket. The gun was half out when Willie sprang.

The knife ripped down Adam's heavy sleeve. It stuck for a moment, and in that moment he swung away. Willie let go of the knife. Adam hit him twice, once on the jaw and once on the nose. Willie's hands came up instinctively. Adam went in and pinned him against the wall, hitting him again and again until he was crumpling, sobbing to himself.

'Enough?' gasped Adam.

Willie rolled slowly forward on to his face and lay there.

Now Adam could turn away.

He said: 'Hello . . . Paula.'

'You know,' she said.

'Yes, we know.'

'Sam as well?'

'Sam as well,' he agreed.

'But . . . you still came for me.'

Her hair stuck out in a weird bristle from the back of her head. Her face was drawn and naked. He took a step towards her, and she stiffened in disbelief as he put his arms round her. Then she went limp and began to cry.

'It's all right,' he murmured. 'It's all over. You're safe.'

'They'll come back. They — '

'I'll be waiting for them,' he promised grimly.

She held on to his lapels and looked wonderingly into his eyes. He kissed her.

'I don't understand,' she sobbed. 'You know who I am. I'm not Barbara Westwood.'

'No. I've met Barbara Westwood.' He grinned. 'I don't think much of her.'

'But — '

'I'm going to take you out to wait in the car,' Adam said. 'You'll be safe out there. Or you can go and have a good meal somewhere while you're waiting.'

'Waiting for what?'

'For the others to come back. I'm staying here to give them a very special reception.'

She looked round the room, and said: 'I'm staying with you.'

'Certainly not.'

'If you take me out now,' she said, 'someone may see us. Then when the others come back, they'll be warned. You'll be in a trap.'

'That's a point. We'll have to be careful when I take you downstairs.'

'It will be safer,' she insisted, 'if we don't move from here. We . . . we can talk. There are things I ought to tell you. I want to talk. I don't want to be alone. I couldn't bear to be left alone now. Not right away.'

Her fingers tightened on his sleeve. Gently he eased her down into the chair by the fire. He saw that she could not be taken out and left in the car or in a restaurant. She was ready to collapse.

He said: 'All right. You can stay. But when they come, keep back. Keep well out of the way. Just in case.'

Her head was bowed. He looked down at her, and knew that there was no escape: frightened and dishevelled as she was, he still found her beautiful and knew that nothing she could tell him would ever make any difference.

Paula said: 'They won't be back for a while, will they?'

'Not for some considerable time, I imagine.'

'You can sit down, then.' A note of

defiance crept into her voice. She put her head back, and the stubbornness in her face made her so like Sam Westwood that it was impossible to believe that she was not his daughter. 'Let me tell you my life story,' she said bleakly. 'It'll pass the time, won't it?'

Willie McKenna stirred and tried to get to his knees. Adam turned to the bed and pulled a sheet off. He lashed Willie's arms behind his back, and tore off a strip to tie his feet together.

Then he said to Paula: 'You don't have to . . . '

'I want you to listen.'

He listened. And all he felt was love. The story she told was the story of somebody else — a shadow figure, a pitiful character out of some tale that had ended long ago. For Paula, too, it was becoming unreal: she faltered, losing conviction.

Adam said: 'You're not telling me your life story at all. You're a very different person from this Paula Hastings you're talking about.'

'Yes,' she marvelled. 'I feel different. Now.'

They sat for a long time in silence: the

321

silence of rest and contentment.

It was broken, at last, by footsteps on the stairs. A voice growled: 'Go on, keep moving. And don't try anything.'

Adam moved swiftly and quietly. He dragged Willie into the lavatory, and stayed there with him. Paula sprawled on the bed. Adam kept the lavatory door slightly ajar. His gun was in his right hand; his left hand rested against the door.

A key turned in the lock of the room door.

'Hey — Willie. Where — '

'He's out,' said Paula blandly.

'Out? What the hell — '

Adam pulled with his left hand; the lavatory door opened and he moved out into the room.

Legat swore, and tensed.

Adam said: 'Stay still. Both of you.'

He heard Paula's sudden cry of dismay, but his attention stayed on Legat and Russell. Even when Russell let go of Sam Westwood so that Sam collapsed to the floor, Adam was not distracted.

'Any guns?' he said tersely.

Legat, his face dark beneath the

sinuous black curls, said: 'Find out.'

'All right. I'll find out. Paula — see what you can do for Sam.'

Paula moved warily round behind the two glowering men. She got her hands under Sam's shoulders, and tried to lift him. He gasped, and got one knee forward. Gradually he pushed himself up. She supported him to the washbasin, and mopped the blood from his face.

'Fine,' he whispered at last, swaying but upright. 'That's fine.'

Adam said: 'See if they've got any guns, will you, Sam?'

'They've got 'em all right.' Sam touched a raw weal across his forehead. 'Where do you think I got this?'

He moved very slowly towards Legat and patted his sides. Then he drew out a revolver and went on to Russell.

Legat said: 'This isn't the end. Don't think it is.'

'I'm afraid it *is*,' Sam said, forcing a smile. It obviously hurt him to smile. 'This is the end, Legat. Russell ought to have told you; Willie ought to have told you: you couldn't win against me.'

He retreated, a gun in each hand. Paula stood close beside him, ready to support him. But he was standing on his own, hunched up, in pain but alive and pleased.

Adam said: 'They tried to beat the truth out of you.'

'They did.'

'But it didn't work.'

'They still don't know where the diamonds are,' Sam confirmed.

Adam studied him with respect. Sam had taken a terrific beating. His eyes were puffy and almost closed; his forehead and cheeks were gashed, and his top lip was swelling into an ugly mass.

'You knew,' said Adam, 'that this would happen.'

'I guessed it would.'

'And — '

'And when they found they couldn't get it out of me,' said Sam, 'I knew what they would do. They weren't going to kill me: that wouldn't have helped one little bit. I was pretty sure they'd bring me back here and . . . try to persuade me by other means.'

Adam looked at Paula, and back at Sam.

Sam nodded. 'Yes. That was the idea. To work over Barbara, as they thought she was, before my eyes. They figured I would talk then.'

'We should both have come here right away. We could have got her out without your taking all that punishment.'

'How were we to know?' said Sam. 'Suppose the address had been wrong? Roger could have been mistaken. Then what would we have done? What would these creatures have done to . . . to Paula if I hadn't turned up at Grenbridge and then gone where they told me on the phone? I had to meet them this time. Then, if you had failed to find her, at least I knew I would be brought along. And somehow or other I'd have beaten them.'

Paula, trembling with fatigue and the aftermath of fear, said: 'Can't we go now? Can't we get out of this place?'

'Yes,' said Sam. 'Let's go.'

Paula led the way out of the room. The two men backed away, watching Legat and Russell.

At the door, Sam said: 'Don't try

anything again. You'll never get those diamonds. Never. You can take my word for that. My word was always pretty good, wasn't it, Russell?'

Russell mouthed something inaudible.

'Forget about the whole business,' Sam concluded. 'Because next time' — there was steel in his voice — 'I won't let you off so easily. Next time my young friend here won't be with me, maybe, and then I won't be so law-abiding. I'll kill you. All three of you. Understood?'

As though hypnotized, Legat and Russell nodded in unison.

Sam and Adam went out, closing the door behind them. They went down the stairs. Paula stood waiting in the doorway, looking out at the cold afternoon with rapture.

Nobody pursued them. There was no sound from above.

'The car's up here,' said Adam. 'Unless,' he added, 'it's been towed away by the police.'

It stood where he had left it. They crowded in, and were silent as the streets opened out into a main road, the road led out through the suburbs, and the suburbs gave way to the countryside. The afternoon darkened over them.

Adam spoke first. He said: 'If you hadn't been able to turn the tables on them . . . if they *had* threatened Paula in front of you — '

'Don't,' said Paula. 'Don't let's talk about it. It didn't happen.'

'If it had happened — '

'It would have been very tricky,' said Sam reflectively.

'You would have given up the diamonds? As a last resort, you'd have given in and told them where the diamonds were?'

'I suppose I would have done. But they wouldn't have been at all pleased. I doubt, even, whether they would have believed me.'

Adam flicked his headlights on. The bright road rushed towards the car, and the hedges, bare and brittle in the winter afternoon, fell away on either side.

He said: 'What did you do with the diamonds?'

'I threw them away,' said Sam. 'The whole lot went to the bottom of the Thames.'

18

'Out of the goodness of my heart,' said Sam, 'I must insist on those diamonds staying where they are. They're no use to you, Adam — and they'd be a great embarrassment to young Mannerlaw.'

He sat in his own chair by his own fireside. In spite of his battered face and hunched, hurt body he looked bigger. There was a new resilience in his voice.

Barbara sat on the edge of the couch. She felt a stranger here. She was, incongruously, no more than an echo of Paula. The impostor had become the real person. Barbara allowed herself to feel amused. She was a visitor who would be leaving tomorrow, and she was no more involved in the things that had happened than if she had been a casual acquaintance: she listened as she might have listened to the account of a family holiday, or a protracted operation.

'Let's just say,' added Sam, 'that all's

well that ends well. And it *has* ended.'

Adam Collier said: 'Damn you, I believe you enjoyed the whole thing. Every little bit of it.'

'No,' said Sam, 'I didn't enjoy it.' He glanced shyly at Paula. 'There was too much at stake.'

'Even so — '

'It meant something to me,' Sam agreed. He flexed his fingers, watching them judicially. 'I . . . I'm remembering what it's like to be alive. It's all coming back.'

'And everything is going to start all over again,' said Barbara, 'just as I said it would.'

Sam accepted her comment as he would have accepted a remark from a visitor — politely, with a little smile that showed she did not understand.

'No,' he said; 'it's not the same as it was. But I can't explain it. Not yet.'

Roger looked from one to the other impatiently. Barbara pursed her lips. She knew what he was thinking, and the little twitch of her mouth told him that she knew. He was longing for somebody to bring up the one important topic. Somebody else, rather than himself. The question was burning him.

Mrs. Westwood cleared her throat, then shook her head wonderingly, and said nothing.

Roger could not restrain himself. He said: 'What did you mean by . . . well, all that stuff about the goodness of your heart?'

Barbara said: 'He means, what about the diamonds?'

'At the bottom of the river,' said Sam placidly.

'But why?'

'The thought of it hurts you, doesn't it?'

'I just want to know,' implored Roger.

Sam stretched his legs. 'I suppose,' he said expansively, 'I owe you all an explanation.'

'It would be very welcome,' said Adam.

Barbara sat back, put her head against the couch cushions, and stared at the far corner of the ceiling. She was interested, no more. Let them get the story finished off, the ends tied up; and tomorrow she would leave.

Sam said: 'In my — ah — more lavish days a certain proportion of my income was derived from regular payments made by people who wished to give some sign of gratitude for my continued discretion.'

'Blackmail?' said Adam.

'The word is generally supposed to have an unpleasant flavour. I can assure you that it is less unpleasant than the things in which these people had been concerned in their time. I saw no reason why they should not pay for their sins. The money was of the greatest use to me, and their monthly payments were a constant reminder to them of the folly of wickedness. One might almost say that I was exercising a very beneficial moral influence on them.'

'What's this got to do with a diamond robbery?' demanded Roger fretfully.

'We're coming to that. One of my most cherished contributors was the Earl of Mannerlaw.'

Adam said: 'Mannerlaw? But ... I don't believe it. He's not the sort to get involved in anything really foul. I had a long talk with him when I took on the job of trying to trace the diamonds through you, and I'm sure he's as straight as they

come. As decent a young fellow as
. . . Oh. I see. You mean the old earl.'

'The old earl,' Sam confirmed. 'The
one who died while I was in prison.'

'I never knew him.'

'You didn't miss anything. I understand
his son is a credit to the family name.
Nobody could have said that about his
father — at least, nobody who knew half
the things *I* did. He frittered away a lot of
his money when he was young, and it
wasn't just boyish exuberance. He was
an unpleasant specimen. There were two
unsavoury incidents at Heidelberg; and
there were some questions about the
death of his first wife that were never
answered. But from my own point of view,
the profitable misdemeanour involved a
Stock Exchange transaction. Perhaps some
of Mannerlaw's fellow directors would have
said that it was an understandable transaction — if not legal, at any rate the sort of
thing that one expects on that battlefield.
Perhaps. But it was a very sharp piece of
dealing, involving two forged documents,
the use of confidential information from a
bank of which he was a director, and the

death of two men. The further results were the suicides of three other men, including one of Mannerlaw's best friends in his own county. Two of them seemed to be accidents rather than suicides; but I had reliable sources of information, and I knew.'

Adam said: 'For a man as rich as Mannerlaw to indulge in that sort of thing — '

'He was not rich. Not nearly as rich as he allowed people to believe. He lived on too lavish a scale, and denied himself nothing. His Stock Exchange manipulation was carried out in order to provide him with funds. It was skilful — but not skilful enough. After he had pulled it off, he had an additional expense — the expense of keeping up my monthly payments.

'He was incapable of lowering his standard of living. He was arrogant and vain, and he had expensive pleasures. Money went very quickly. And even if he could have started, at that stage, to make economies, he still had to meet my demands. If he didn't, I could have ruined him — not only financially, but in the eyes of all the people whose flattery meant so much to him. He had to keep me quiet. Once he tried to have me killed. After that I raised the figure for his contributions.

'With all these demands on his pocket, he had to do something. During the war, he approached me and asked for my help. It was for our mutual benefit. If I wanted him to keep up his payments, I would have to do some work for him. He thought I could be trusted. He was right. I was to dispose of the Mannerlaw diamonds for him. Quietly, without fuss, at the highest price I could get for them. He thought I would make a better job of it than anyone else he knew. Again he was right. I got rid of them, handed over the money — less a small commission — and he was able to go on paying me the — ah — fines for his folly.'

Adam's jaw dropped. 'You . . . *sold* the Mannerlaw diamonds?'

'Bit by bit. The main pieces were broken up, of course. No word ever leaked out.'

'In that case the robbery — '

'The robbery,' said Sam, 'was visualized, right from the beginning, as part of our plan. It was settled that after the war, when the Mannerlaw valuables were brought back to London — as they'd have to be — I would be responsible for removing the fakes. The earl would then claim the insurance. That way he would get the money for the diamonds twice over — and, of course, be able to go on paying me. That's what we agreed; and that's what I did.'

'And you were the only two who knew the diamonds weren't real?'

'The earl and myself knew; and he's dead now.'

'The men who worked for you . . . ?'

'They worked for me,' said Sam flatly. 'That was that. I paid them for the job, and the rest of it was no concern of theirs.'

'But they didn't see it that way,' said Adam.

Sam's grin was rueful, but still arrogant and unrepentant. 'I had a mutiny on my hands,' he admitted. 'They ganged up on me and said they wanted a bigger cut. I told them they weren't going to get one. I ran the show, and they took what I offered them. I never stood for argument. Then it all blew up — one of them talked after I'd beaten him up — and the police were on to us fast.'

'You couldn't have told them — '

'The truth?' Sam shook his head. 'In the first place I wouldn't have trusted them with details of my relations with Mannerlaw. They'd have tried to cash in on that, too: they'd have wrecked the whole set-up. That's why I went along on that job myself. And in the second place, I wasn't going to be pushed around by scum like that. I ran the show,' he said again; 'it wasn't up to me to explain things to men who merely worked for me.'

'You didn't consider telling the police the real story when you were arrested?'

'No,' said Sam, 'I didn't. The robbery with violence was just as real, fakes or no fakes. And there wasn't any sense in bringing old Mannerlaw down with me. He could still lay quite a lot of golden eggs for me, one day! It was just a pity that he died while I was still inside. When I got out I couldn't take up where I'd left off. Young Mannerlaw was different stuff from his father — and in any case, with death duties he had precious little left.

Even before I got out I knew that nothing was going to be the same.'

It was Roger who concluded the story for his father. 'So the diamonds are gone. The real ones — and the fakes.'

'As soon as I'd got my hands on the fakes,' said Sam, 'I disposed of them. They're in the river; and they'll never be found.'

Roger's despair drew his cheeks down, turned the corners of his mouth down, and blurred like tears in his eyes. Then, abruptly, he began to laugh. It was a strange, warped sound in the quiet room. For a moment it verged on hysteria; and then it became the laughter of relief — as though something was over and done with, and there was no point in worrying any more.

'I don't know what I'm going to do now,' he said weakly, but still laughing.

Barbara said: 'I know what *I'm* going to do. I'm going to go to bed, and first thing in the morning I'll be off.' She looked at Paula. 'I wanted to see what my — my other self was like. Now I've seen it, there's nothing to stay for. There's nothing here for me.' She swung towards her father. 'Is there?'

'No,' said Sam very gently, 'there's nothing here for you.' He studied her for a long moment. 'I rather like you,' he said. 'You've got guts. And one hell of a stiff neck.'

Barbara gave a slight, histrionic shudder.

Paula said: 'Please, you must — '

'We've got a lot of sorting out to do,' said Sam, talking her down. Barbara was grateful to him. She wanted no emotion, no urgent appeals. 'Things haven't been normal here. Now perhaps they can be. We can take our time. We can do things quietly . . . get to know one another.' He was not looking at his wife, but there was a faint dry note of something like humility in his voice. 'There's a lot to be done,' he said.

Adam got up and thrust his hands into his pockets. 'You're right there.' He stared gloomily down at Sam's head. 'How the blazes am I going to report back on this? It'll be the devil of a job to persuade my folk that there aren't any Mannerlaw diamonds any more.'

'And if you succeed in doing so,' rapped Sam, 'all you'll do will be to make things extremely unpleasant for young Mannerlaw. I don't know what action your insurance company would take in such circumstances — but I'm convinced Mannerlaw would be the one who'd come out of it worst. That's one reason why I said the fake diamonds should stay where they are, and be forgotten.'

'Out of the goodness of your heart!' Adam quoted sardonically. 'But what do I say? Just that I've been unable to trace the confounded things — '

'And don't believe anybody ever *will* trace them.'

'I wouldn't feel happy about doing that.'

'Oh, my God.' Sam ran one hand through his hair. 'Another stiff-necked one!'

'And if I marry Paula, and it gets out — as it will — that she's been connected with you — '

'Who says you're going to marry her?'

Adam looked across the room into Paula's eyes. They met his gaze and held it.

He said: 'I say so.'

'Not yet,' said Sam. 'She's going to stay

here for a while, until I'm sure you're good enough for her.' He glanced tenderly at Paula's shock of gashed hair. 'I want her to myself for a little while,' he said.

'Now look here . . . '

Barbara got up, yawning. 'Bed for me,' she said. 'What time is there a train from Easterdyke in the morning?'

'There's a seven-thirty,' said Roger. 'I'll run you in to the station,' he added eagerly.

'And get rid of me?'

'Speed you on your way,' he said with acid pleasure.

She went towards the door. There were polite good nights. She looked back at them all once, as she opened the door. They all looked far away. She was detached from them, and glad to be so. Yet there was *something* . . .

Something she would not admit was envy. As the door closed she was aware that they were building up between them a tangled, exasperating relationship that offered possibilities she would never know. It made no sense. There were no values here, no standards.

They were creating something to which

she could not belong.

When she lay in bed she could hear the companionable buzz of their voices rising from below. They were still talking as she drifted off into sleep.

Tomorrow she would get back to her neat, sensible life, away from these people who were always making difficulties for themselves — the blunderers, the clumsy ones. They would never learn. This time she would not come back. She did not even want to know what happened to them.

She slept, sure of herself. The others, less sure, stayed volubly awake for a long time.

THE END

We do hope that you have enjoyed reading this large print book.

Did you know that all of our titles are available for purchase?

We publish a wide range of high quality large print books including:
Romances, Mysteries, Classics
General Fiction
Non Fiction and Westerns

Special interest titles available in large print are:
The Little Oxford Dictionary
Music Book, Song Book
Hymn Book, Service Book

Also available from us courtesy of Oxford University Press:
Young Readers' Dictionary
(large print edition)
Young Readers' Thesaurus
(large print edition)

For further information or a free brochure, please contact us at:
Ulverscroft Large Print Books Ltd.,
The Green, Bradgate Road, Anstey,
Leicester, LE7 7FU, England.
Tel: (00 44) 0116 236 4325
Fax: (00 44) 0116 234 0205

VICTORIAN VILLAINY

Michael Kurland

Professor James Moriarty stands alone as the particular nemesis of Sherlock Holmes. But just how evil was he? Here are four ingenious stories, all exploring an alternate possibility: that Moriarty wasn't really a villain at all. But why, then, did Holmes describe Moriarty as 'the greatest schemer of all time', and 'the Napoleon of crime'? Holmes could never *catch* Moriarty in any of his imagined schemes — which only reinforced his conviction that the professor was, indeed, an evil genius . . .

THE DYRYSGOL HORROR AND OTHER STORIES

Edmund Glasby

What is the nature of the evil that terrorises Dyrysgol? Detective Inspector Bernard Owen's investigation involves people disappearing from this remote Welsh village. Local anger is directed towards Dyrysgol Castle and its enigmatic owner. But whilst Viscount Ravenwood is a little strange, is he a murderer? Then another man goes missing and his car is left with great claw marks across the roof, as Owen and his officers are dragged towards the bloody conclusion of the mystery of Dyrysgol . . .

WHITE JADE

V. J. Banis

Chris Channing's former fiancé Jeff tells her that his life is in danger: his wife is slowly poisoning him. But is this true? Responding to his claim, Chris goes to him at Morgan House where she's up against the strange brother-in-law David, the cunning wife Mary, and Jeff, the man she'd once loved, but who's now vastly changed. Chris, lost, confused and swept into a powerful undertow of danger, begins to realize that someone is trying to kill her . . .

THE NIGHTMARE WHISPERERS

John Burke

The Gifted Ones have the uncanny ability to enter into people's dreams and control them, implanting subconscious ideas, invoking nightmares. As boys, Dominic Lynch and Patrick Robson were kept as virtual prisoners and their skills exploited for military purposes. When Patrick escapes, it's only to another kind of prison. However, his talent is used for corporate espionage, although he has his own agenda. Yet neither man can escape the corruption their power brings.